Galactically Speaking

Galactically Speaking

by

Fred J. Klingenhagen

FirstPublish
A Division of the Brskol Group, Inc.
control your own destiny

ISBN
1-929925-67-0

Library of Congress Cataloging in Publication Data
2001090030

Fred J. Klingenhagen
Galactically Speaking

10 9 8 7 6 5 4 3 2 1

FIRSTPUBLISH
A Division of Brekel Group, Inc.
300 Sunport Ln.
Orlando, FL 32809
407-240-1414
www.firstpublish.com

DATE: September 11, 2054

NUMBER OF PAGES: 185 (including cover sheet)

TO:
Name: Julie Ryan
Company: AT&T/MCI Educational Research Center
Address: Area 51, Suite 1356
                       Sprint City, Gangis Chasma
                       Mars
Telephone: (4457) 8923-75-9832#60
Fax: (4457) 8993-21-4573#61

FROM:

Name: Leddie Fennhadden
Company: N/A
Address: Rt 2 Box 143
                       Cedar Key, Florida
                       U.S.A., Earth
Telephone: (3378) 9932-61-3969#71
Fax: (3378) 9923-16-2875#72

GREETINGS TO MY all-time favorite interplanetary niece on her (my God!) 74th birthday. I wasn't able to send this transmission via I-Mail because there are just too many pages —- had to use the old-fashioned quantum fax. (Talk about primitive.)

Say hello to everyone in the family for me and be sure to give your grandson, a/k/a the "Little Space Buckaroo," a great big kiss. Although I don't get to see you guys as much as I'd like, I think it's great we live in an era where people can work in interplanetary space. It's so —- 21st century.

I tried tracking down the box of stuff I sent you for Christmas, but from what I can gather (after nine months and about a dozen sub-space transmissions), your presents are still floating around some-where within the deep, dark recesses of the Port Tranquillity Postal Service Center.

Your Mom probably told you we were finally able to crowbar your Dad off his hover-yacht and the two of them came down to Cedar Key for her 100th birthday. At first, we tried using our powers of persuasion on your dear father and, when that didn't work, we bribed him with broiled lobster at Cheap Chet's Crabshackle.

It was a very relaxing long weekend —- translation: we didn't do a ding-dang thing except lounge around on the porch, go out to Chet's for your Mom's birthday dinner and stroll down to the Gulf for sunset.

Over cake and coffee, your parents and I started reminiscing and we realized it's been twenty years since your Uncle Nick was killed in that damn VentureStar accident. Thank goodness they've made commercial space travel a lot safer since then.

We also decided that the three of us weren't getting any younger and figured it was time to tell you the truth about your Uncle Nick. It's a story we've never told anyone for reasons that'll soon be made clear. We felt it was important to pass this family secret on to you before we are also gone and it's lost forever.

I've never considered myself much of a writer, but I've always been an avid reader and the following narrative is based on my old diary journals, transcripts from a dicto-disc recording your Dad and Nick made about a year before the accident, other people's —- not a precise term —- remembrances, some confidential computer logs and a little literary license. (Although with me, it's more like a literary learner's permit.) You'll also notice I decided to refer to your Father by name throughout most of the text because, halfway through the second draft, I got sick of writing: "your Dad" did this, "your Dad" said that, all the time.

These events took place in December, 2005 and January, 2006 when you were away at Virginia Tech (grad school, if memory serves) and your Mom was finishing her final tour of duty at Camp Lejeune.

Finally (and this was a unanimous decision), your parents and I agreed to leave it up to you to decide when the time would be right for you to tell the kids, grandkids and possibly the rest of the human race about what happened.

So Julie, here goes …

Chapter 1

TWO POINT, ONE four seconds to wormhole expulsion," the Bablona 66-L shipboard computer reported in a sultry voice that would be the envy of any self-respecting phone sex operator.

The starcraft surged forward along the wormhole's hypersurface in a blaze of white-hot light, passed through its exit portal and lurched back into normal space-time.

To recreate the spatial and temporal disorientation caused by the skewed multi-dimensional geometric plane of a wormhole, just have someone sneak up from behind and push you into a pool of freezing water. That comes pretty close.

"Reduce to half light speed," the pilot ordered.
The breaking thrusters fired, the ultra-light drive disengaged and the ship used an entire light year to decelerate to a mere 143,000 miles per second.

"Point five light speed," the computer acknowledged.

The Bablona 66-L (a vast improvement over its predecessor, the 56-K model) was a highly advanced galactic computer designed specifically for interstellar commercial starcraft. It provided navigation and communication functions, monitored propulsion and inertial systems and maintained internal environment and life support. It also had virtually unlimited data storage and retrieval capability. Its most distinctive feature, however, was a voice modem that sounded just like sexy actress Holli Daye when she played the sadistic serial killer in that old mystery movie: "Murder Takes the

Fifth." (In actuality, the computer's voice was provided by a famous female quantum-golfer from Regulon V named Zarena).

At half the speed of light, the giant planet Jupiter was just a momentary red blip on the forward viewscreen as the starcraft streaked toward its target coordinates.

"How long until we reach the planet's atmosphere?" the pilot asked.

"At present speed, fifty-eight seconds," the computer replied.

"Switch to manual control."

"Disengaging computer navigation."

The pilot took a healthy slug of Twany Blend Expresso from the snazzy new anti-gravity mug his boss had given him for the Sacred Feast of Xylos. He eased his control column forward and the ship plunged into the yellow fire of Earth's atmosphere.

Twany Blend was a rare, exotic and very fashionable coffee that had the look and consistency of molten 14-karat gold and packed a caffeine jolt that would throw a human metabolism into anaphylactic shock. It was grown exclusively in the remote tundra regions of a planet called Maris IX, located somewhere out and to the left of the constellation Capricorn.

"Begin audio program," the pilot said.

The twangy opening guitar riff to Chuck Berry's "Around and Around" erupted over the comm-system and filled the cockpit with what is considered by many beings throughout galactic space to be the ideal soundtrack for an interstellar joyride.

Unbeknownst to most of the civilized galaxy, there is a lonely stretch of swampy lowlands located between the Banana River and Florida State Road 256-A that, under the right conditions, provides a visual spectacle to rival the famous Helium Caves of Anterious and the Great Cobalt Reef on Perxis IV (two of this star sector's leading tourist destinations).

The chilly winter temperatures, just before sunrise, strike the warm inland river and the water condenses, producing a blanket of voluminous fog that shrouds the entire area in a ghostly gray mist. Stately groves of Sabal Palm trees, most of them thirty to forty feet high, are reduced to gigantic surrealistic mushrooms growing in a meadow of smoky vapor (think of Jurassic Period Earth, and throw in an all-out L.A. smog alert). As the sun rises, the horizon slowly turns from midnight blue to bright purple, and transforms the entire area an other-worldly shade of lavender. It looks like a Dali painting without the melted clock.

Flying a small craft slow and low (say — three hundred miles an hour at an altitude of fifty feet) over this bizarre landscape makes for an exhilarating ride.

The starship broke through the crimson fire at the lower rim of atmosphere, blasted through the heavy layer of alto-cumulus cloud cover and nose-dived toward the ocean of pea soup. The pilot glanced up from his instrument panel at the forward viewscreen and spotted the ghost-like wisps of steam billowing up from the surface of the river.

He cut his control column to the left and the ship performed a sharp, rolling dive straight for the widest bend in the winding, serpentine river. He popped the breaking thruster switch, slowing the ship to a mere two hundred miles an hour, and leveled off over the water. He then jerked the column sharply to the right for just a split second. The starboard fusion thruster peppered the river like a Tommy gun, launching a massive wall of brownish-green spray into the air.

"Babs, we are definitely cruis—in' now," the pilot said with a smile.

"Affirmative," the computer acknowledged. "Please define: 'cruis—in'."

"I'll tell you later."

Inspired by Chuck Berry's second chorus (which had something to do with having the joint: a-rockin'), and the weird panorama flashing by on the viewer, the pilot smirked with satisfaction as he maneuvered the ship over the purple mist, deftly dodging palm tree toadstools as he flew.

He took another sip of expresso and made a strafing run on a large patch of tall Sabals growing along the river bank. He spun the control column hard to starboard, punched the thrust accelerators and the ship barrel-rolled past the tree canopy. Its afterburners fired a volley of fusion exhaust, ignited the dry fronds on the tops of the trees and they burst into flames. The pilot took another sip off his mug, jerked back on the column and the ship climbed. He doubled back to check his handiwork — a 40-foot high psychedelic bonfire blazing amid a sea of gray gas.

"Cool beans."

"Affirmative. I believe we have achieved: 'cooliousity'."

"You're learning, Babs."

The pilot was clearly peaking when Bablona, in a throaty voice that sounded like it would break into a chorus of "Happy Birthday Mr. President," informed him that the right rear lift stabilizer had malfunctioned.

The starship pitched to port and ricocheted off the top of the tallest Sabal.

"Jumpin' Jupiter!" he yelped as the glancing blow buffeted the small craft. "Reroute power to the lift stabilizer."

"Reserve power to stabilizer: negative function."

"Switch to secondary hydraulics!" he barked as Chuck Berry wailed something about learning to dance.

"Secondary hydraulics are not engaging," the computer said. "I believe we will be forced to discontinue 'cruis—in'."

The ship leveled off momentarily, then suddenly pitched to the left, knocking the pilot's anti-gravity mug off the primary instrument console and into midair.

"Engage automatic navigation."

The mug hovered about a foot off the forward deck directly in front of the Internal Environment display readout, but the ship plunged into the fog, second-guessing the computer's command.

"Automatic navigation system is not engaging."

The sudden drop in altitude caused the bottom of the ship to scrape the tops of several tall palms and jar the small craft again.

"Hell's Bells!" the pilot cried. Frantically, he flipped the manual override switch on and off, on and off, but the automatic navigation system refused to engage. He glanced up at the forward viewscreen just in time to see two massive tree trunks filling the forward viewscreen very quickly. He yanked the column hard to port and the ship swerved, missing the palm tree uprights by inches.

This maneuver, while averting certain catastrophe, forced the ship out of the palm groves and over State Road 256-A. It blasted down the highway only a few feet above the pavement at about two hundred miles an hour heading straight for a GMAC Jimmy Sport Utility Vehicle.

"Increase altitude immediately," Bablona suggested in what would be considered in most circumstances a very sensuous whisper. The pilot yanked back on his control column and the ship buzzed my truck, clearing it by about six inches, but the heat from the fusion thrusters seared the paint off my roof. Asshole!

Following the third near-miss in as many seconds, the ship's console lights flashed off, helm control went dead and the ship plummeted out of the sky, careening on its fuselage into an embankment of soft sand about fifty yards from the highway.

It bounced twice, rolled three times and miraculously came to rest on its belly amid a patch of palm stumps and scrub palmetto.

Chuck Berry's guitar solo kicked in on the comm-system monitor as the pilot, still strapped in his seat, head bowed and body straining against the safety harness, promptly blacked out.

Chapter 2

I WAS ABOUT halfway to work, driving my brand new (well, new to me) GMAC Jimmy, when I encountered the strange charcoal gray aircraft that looked like a cross between a Learjet and a Stealth Bomber.

My hands were shaking as I pulled onto the shoulder of State Road 256-A and rolled to a stop.

"Great," I griped, my chest heaving with adrenaline, "our tax dollars at work."

I watched the trail of smoke rising above the downed craft, trying to figure out what the hell an Air Force jet was doing buzzing around out here in the middle of nowhere. After a few deep breaths to calm down, I decided I'd better go see if anybody was hurt and in need of assistance.

Fortunately, the jet didn't crash too far from the road and my Jimmy's four-wheel drive could easily handle the sandy terrain. I jammed the truck in gear, hung a left across the highway and plunged into the scrub. The SUV bounced along on the soft sand as I carefully maneuvered around palm trees and patches of palmetto and scrub oak. I pulled up to within a few feet of the strange jet and stopped.

I had never seen anything like it — even on the evening news — but it looked like something those marbleheads in Congress would've spent billions to develop only to find it didn't work. The weird craft was about twice the size of a private plane and made of a strange, dark gray metallic alloy. The hull was shaped like a "W" with a mini-version of the space shuttle attached to the top. A green running light on the tip of the left wing was blinking on and off like a forgotten turn signal. It didn't seem to be burning; the rising fumes of black smoke merely exhaust residue.

I got out of the truck and slowly edged toward the wrecked plane. As I neared the strange craft, I could make out a single silhouette through the cockpit window and heard muted strains of "Around and Around" playing inside. I wrinkled my nose and raised a perplexed eyebrow.

"Chuck Berry?"

At that instant, the cockpit hatch released sending me reeling. I lost my balance, fell backward and landed on my butt, narrowly missing a palm stump. Fortunately, I've got a lot of padding down there. The hatch rose in slow motion revealing a single male pilot still strapped in his seat. Dazed, he looked at me but did not speak.

"Are you alright?" I asked, getting up, dusting off my bottom and inching forward a few steps. "Are you hurt?"

"B — Babs, is that you?" the pilot sputtered. He was pretty groggy but didn't seem to be injured; at least he wasn't bleeding or anything. He shook his head a few times and tried to focus.
He began to emerge from his crash-induced funk and stared at me with a glazed expression on his face.

"You sound just like Bablona."

"Who's Bablona?" I asked. "For that matter, who are you?"

The pilot switched off the music, yanked off his safety harness and slowly climbed out of the cockpit.

I backed up a few steps.

He was tall and slender, just under six feet tall, with a boyish face, although he looked to be around forty. He had brown hair, long enough to curl over the tops of his ears, and almond-colored eyes.

He turned around, put his hands on his hips and surveyed his craft.

"Just goes to show that Deklaan's Principle has never been more valid," he said.

"Dek-laan's Principle?"

"Whatever can go wrong — will go wrong."

"You mean Murphy's Law."

"It's a universal concept."

We just stood there for the next few awkward moments inspecting the damage. I craned my neck around the stranger to get a better look at the interior of the weird-looking craft. Much to my surprise, it looked a lot like the cockpit of a commercial jet liner, except for the twin hatches that swung up and out like the doors on a Ferrari Berlinetta. Inside were two high-backed, very comfortable looking, Barcolounger-like chairs, presumably for a pilot and a co-pilot. Unlike a jet, only the chair on the right (must be a British-made craft) had a control column sticking up from the floor directly in front of it with twin joy-stick controls on top. There were control consoles dividing the cockpit in half and lining the arms of both chairs. The consoles were covered with hundreds of buttons, switches, indicator lamps and instrument readouts. The dashboard, for lack of a better word, contained a dozen or so video display terminals for registering God-knows-what, although one of the screens seemed to have some type of map or chart on it. The windows on the hatches and the windshield didn't seem to be windows at all, but rather some type of high-resolution viewscreen that reminded me of those night vision goggles the military used during the Persian Gulf War.

"I've never seen a jet like this before. And — I've never heard of Air Force pilots cruising around listening to rock and roll."

It suddenly occurred to me that the pilot wasn't wearing any type of uniform or flight suit. On the contrary, he had on faded Levi's, sneakers and a red T-shirt emblazoned with "Green Parrot Bar" on the front and "See the Keys on Your Hands and Knees" on back.

"I'm not affiliated with the military."

"No kidding."

"Are you alright?"

"Yes, I'm fine," I replied, surprised by his concern. "What about you?"

Something was very odd here. The stranger was polite, articulate and, in a rumpled sort of way, kinda cute — there was definitely something fishy about him.

"If you're running drugs, I don't even want to know about it!".

As if on cue, a driver-side airbag exploded inside the cockpit. It inflated instantaneously, proudly displaying the Chrysler Corporation logo.

"Leapin' Lizards!" the pilot cried.

"Leap—ing Lizards?" I muttered to myself. O—kay, what planet did this clown just blow in from?

"Just in time to prevent serious bodily injury," he said, with a smirk. "Actually, these airbags are one of your better inventions."

"Wait a minute — what do you mean one of MY better inventions?"

"Not you personally, yours as a species."

"Who the hell are you?"

The strange guy paused, arched an eyebrow and looked like he was in the process of cooking up a real doozy.

"My name's Ithran Nek-Hånån. I'm originally from a planet called Selrahc, which is located a couple hundred light years beyond what you know as the Taurus star group.

"Why am I not surprised?"

"However," he continued, in a conversational tone, "you here on Earth refer to me by another name."

I rolled my eyes and folded my arms. I was right about the doozy.

"Okay, buster — what's your Earth alias?"

"God."

Chapter 3

MEREK, EVER-PRESENT comm-unit under one arm, chugged his portly frame up the countless ivory brick steps leading to the entrance of the Regional Council Hall located on Baltrus VII.

The planet of Baltrus VII was an extraordinarily beautiful world blessed with the best weather in the galaxy and it was certainly no coincidence the Galactic Association of Star Systems (GASS) chose it for the site of its regional headquarters. If highly-placed galactic officials were required to leave their home worlds to live and work on a distant planet, then the warm sunshine and idyllic temperatures provided by Baltrus's binary star system was the only way to go.

The Regional Council Hall was an imposing hexagonal-shaped structure encased entirely in translucent aquamarine hydro-glass. A dozen stories tall, the building's interiors featured majestic cathedral ceilings and glossy purple Alterian marble floors.
This magnificent piece of interstellar architecture made the Palace of Versailles look like a Sabrett's hot dog wagon.

Winded and perspiring, Merek paused on the top step to catch his breath. He gazed out at the lavish botanical gardens surrounding the Hall that contained acres of exotic flora collected from all corners of the known galaxy.

Middle-aged (5500 in Earth years) and humanoid physically, Merek was from the frontier planet of Beor (go a couple of light years past Sirius, and hang a left — you can't miss it). He was of average size for males of his species, six foot tall and weighing three hundred and fifty pounds. His round, pleasant face featured chubby cheeks and kind eyes topped off with salt-and-pepper hair. He was soft-spoken, in an absent-minded professor sort of way, and possessed a self-deprecating sense of humor that could charm friend and foe alike. The blue-tinted triangular bifocals he wore perched on the tip of his nose had earned him the nickname, "Professor Pudge." (Merek had a rare form of Beoran astigmatism that could not be corrected by positron laser surgery.)

A vice president on the Association organizational chart, Merek was head of the Problem Planet Department, which managed a portfolio of over three thousand problem worlds and employed one hundred Problem Planet Administrators plus support staff.

He was, as usual, late for his audience with the Regional Council, which was not surprising because Merek was always late for something. This propensity for tardiness was not due to negligence on his part but rather logistics — Merek's department was responsible for monitoring and maintaining problem planets stretching over one-third of the known galaxy (about 40 thousand light years — or 400 trillion square miles).

He bustled through the automatic doors of the Council Hall's hydrolift, crossed the marbled foyer and legged it down a red, neon-tube-lined corridor (sort of interstellar Art Deco decor) that led into the Regional Council Chambers.

Seated behind one of two large slab tables carved from very rare (and expensive) GoGanian Ebony was Azor-Zadok Velitel. A native of Selrahc, Velitel was a rough and ready being in both appearance and demeanor — a sort of galactic Marlboro Man. He had spent decades exploring the asteroid belts surrounding the Zaavan Nebula and hunting Wooly Mammoth on Bekka III. Despite these hearty extracurricular activities, he was an attorney by trade, his specialty: Galactic Association Law. Merek utilized him as a consultant whenever departmental legal affairs got — complicated.

"I missed you at dinner last night," Velitel said in lieu of a greeting.

"I was stuck on Ferrris until late."

Velitel had been fortunate enough to catch the early subspace transport and spent the evening dining on rich Vagan cuisine, washing it down with a very fine Negahnegnilkian Chardonnay.

Stuck on Ferrris in a dispute with planetary zoning officials, Merek arrived on Baltrus VII with only enough time to race over to the Council Hall directly from the star shuttle port.

"Aren't the Ferrris that symbionic species?" Velitel asked.

"That's right," the big Beoran groaned. "And that makes negotiating with them extremely difficult — they keep changing their minds!"

"The chardonnay was an excellent 4445 vintage."

"I don't want to hear it. I ate star shuttle food."

"Tough break."

"If we're finished with the culinary treatise, may we please begin?"

This curt request came from Kothan, Senior Vice-President of the Regional Galactic Council. He and his two fellow members, both Executive V.P.'s, had slipped into the Chambers through a secured rear entrance. The Council consisted of: Kothan, a native of the planet Moogalie; Jidlaph, a Pahoogalian from the same solar system; and Uz who hailed from a mysterious, isolated world called Kreggor.

Kothan and Jidlaph were indistinguishable from humans except for their skin colors, which were subdued shades of blue and red, respectively. Uz was a three foot, six inch tall, bear-like creature covered head to toe with coarse brown fur.

Kothan and Jidlaph wore pastel golf shirts with the "GASS" emblem over the left pocket and khaki slacks, the customary garb of Association officials.

Casual dress had been in vogue for centuries (for those species that wore clothes), after a galaxy-wide sociological study determined informal, comfortable clothing was extremely helpful in fostering peaceful relations among interstellar species.

Uz wore nothing at all as was conventional for Kreggorians. Fortunately for the others present, his heavy coat of thick fur hid everything that could be considered embarrassing.

The trio sat behind a 12-inch thick slab altar also carved from the same GoGanian Ebony. It was equipped with three data-comm terminals and sat on a raised platform that allowed the Council to lord over a gallery consisting of a dozen rows of church pew-like benches sculpted out of white Xoian Jade (which was not as expensive and hard to come by, but was really cool looking). A wide middle aisle divided the tables and the gallery.

Kothan sat in the middle, flanked on the right by Jidlaph with Uz seated to his left. All three had dark scowls on their faces. Uz stood up, although it was hard to tell, and began without preliminaries.

"It has come to the attention of the Regional Council that one of the Problem Planet Administrators in your department is in violation of Sections 518.85 and 1226.58: Galactic Policies and Procedures."

Merek furrowed his brow and leaned over to confer with his long-time companion.

"Those sections prohibit interstellar contact with Class-D designated planets and forbids interfering with their social evolutionary development," Velitel whispered. They broke off their conversation to hear Jidlaph's voice thunder throughout the Council Chambers.

"Those are not all — nor are they the most serious violations to be addressed!" he bellowed, grabbing the spotlight away from Uz who gave him a short, derisive grunt before reluctantly re-taking his seat.

Jidlaph paused for a self-aggrandizing moment while Merek and Velitel hunched forward, their elbows propped up on the table and their minds racing with fearful anticipation.

"Get on with it while the millennium's still young!" Kothan ordered, while he punched something on his comm-screen.

The sister worlds of Moogalie and Pahoogalie not only produced two out of the three Regional Council members, but also one of the more curious sociological histories known to the Association. Both planets revolved around a giant yellow star called Sarn 121, located on the outskirts of the Brax Nebula. Separated by a mere fifty-five million miles, the two planetary societies evolved alongside one another dreaming of the day when they would make actual physical contact.

Within a few millennia, both worlds were communicating via radio and television transmissions and from there, they began directing their shared scientific research toward the singular goal of achieving interplanetary space flight.

Several centuries later, their combined technology had advanced to the point where safe, manned space travel had been developed and the Moogalie-Pahoogalie Interplanetary Space Administration (MPISA) devised a master plan calling for space vehicles to be launched simultaneously from each world. Astronauts from Moogalie would land on their sister world at the same time a Pahoogalian ship would arrive on Moogalie.

The coordinated operation worked to perfection with both spacecraft landing within minutes of each other to the thunderous applause of billions of spectators. The two sister civilizations had finally achieved their centuries-old dream of interplanetary contact.

This historic event was immediately followed by centuries of dissension, bickering and extraterrestrial conflict.

Both species soon began to consider the other flawed – inferior physically, intellectually, spiritually, and in some ways proper decorum prohibits mentioning. In the words of the renowned Mahoogalian philosopher, Parthag: "Too much familiarity gets irritating." Tensions ran so high at one point that both world governments agreed to collaborate on a project, which involved the nuclear detonation of an uninhabited moon. (The first thing they had agreed upon in over three hundred years.) The fragments caused by the explosion formed an asteroid belt that would forever separate the two feuding planets. (Of course, in the heat of the moment, no one considered the possibility of just flying around the asteroids.)

It wasn't until the highly advanced and incredibly fashionable inhabitants of Pyxis III made that sector's first interstellar contact that the squabbling sister worlds begrudgingly made peace.

The Pyxis were accomplished astronauts and skilled stellar cartographers who had explored their vast regions of space for thousands of years. They had successfully charted hundreds of star systems and also discovered several of the more strategically located wormholes.

The Pyxis were also considered to be the coolest, hippest beings in the galaxy.

Much to the Moogalies and Pahoogalies surprise and chagrin, the Pyxis became enamored with the purple-hued, cross-bred descendants of both planets. Known as Koloncdonks (literally translated as "those people"), they were objects of scorn on their respective home worlds. The Pyxis, however, considered them to be one of the most intelligent and attractive races they had encountered in nearly seven millennia of galactic exploration. According to the Pyxis, the Koloncdonks were one of only a handful of species to possess natural cooliousity (the capacity to be "cool").

The Moogalies and Pahoogalies, fearing they would seem unenlightened and, worse, unfashionable, to the newly arrived interstellar hipsters, not only reconciled their planetary differences but also lovingly embraced the now "too cool" Koloncdonks.

Species as shallow and superficial as the Moogalies and Pahoogalies were perfectly suited for elected office.

"Can the Regional Council expound on the nature of these charges?" Velitel countered.

Jidlaph paused, then sighed — a long, dramatic sigh. He loved an audience – any audience.

"First the lesser charges." He paused and sighed again.

An impatient Kothan cut him off in the interest of time. Jidlaph mumbled something that sounded like "Mister Big Shot" and, with an indignant snort, sat back down.

"Approximately 1400 B.C., Earth Calendar, the Israelites, a primitive tribe of humans — fleeing their captors, the Egyptians — were miraculously saved from wholesale massacre by the unnatural disruption of a large inland body of water known as the —," Kothan had to pause to consult his comm-screen — "the Red Sea — which stood between them and escape."

The Senior V.P. glowered at the two seated before him. Velitel leaned over and pretended to confer with Merek on a procedural point to escape his lethal glare.

"Although noble in intent, this action was nonetheless a serious violation of Association policy."

"Furthermore," Jidaph jumped in as Kothan took a moment to punch something else up on his data-comm unit, "during the next millennium, extraterrestrials from three Association worlds were surreptitiously placed into the primitive Earth population in order to profess alternative religious doctrines." He, too, had to refer to his screen. "Jesus, Mohammed and Buddha, as they were known to the human cultures of their day, were considered divinely-inspired entities sent to Earth by a benevolent supreme being to instruct them in matters of a spiritual nature." Jidlaph paused for dramatic effect. "Grievous, gratuitous, vio—,"

"Finally, the most serious of the charges," Uz announced, cutting the galactic windbag off in mid-sentence, "Capital Murder of a Class-D Species Being!"

Merek and Velitel's jaws dropped so fast they almost banged the slab table top as the incredible charge reverberated throughout the council chambers.

"Capital Murder!" they gasped in stereo.

Violent crimes were virtually unheard of among the higher echelons of sentient life inhabiting Association worlds (Class A through C species designations). The strict policy prohibiting interplanetary contact with what were perceived as less evolved life forms was considered the primary reason for this peaceful galactic environment.

"Obviously, we're going to need the Council's complete file on this and the other charges in order to investigate these matters fully." Velitel waxed legal.

Jidlaph was about to respond when Kothan waved him off.

"In the latter part of the twentieth century, Earth Calendar, the assassination of a Class-D species being, one J. Fitzgerald Kennedy – a planetary head of state — no less — was commissioned, planned and orchestrated by the defendant with what possible motive or intent the Council is — at this time — unaware." (A lot of aliens talk like this.)

Kothan pressed a control on his data-comm console. "I am accessing full reports on these and all the allegations for your review."

He popped another control. "And, restricting any further departmental communications with the defendant."

"Capital Murder — I can't believe it," Merek muttered, shaking his head.

Although he managed over a hundred Problem Planet Administrators, and there were always questions of policy adherence to address (the Association Concurrence Department could be very persnickety), he knew all of his staff very well and couldn't, in his wildest dreams, imagine any of his employees capable of killing another sentient being.

It was just not done in galactic life form circles.

"Let's cut to re-entry and touch down, shall we?" Velitel counterpunched. "Who is charged with these offenses?"

"Ithran Nek-Hånån!"

Chapter 4

WELL, YOU CERTAINLY don't have a problem with self-esteem," I said, not taking the stranger's claim of being the Almighty the least bit seriously. Why would God need a spacecraft to get around? "I don't suppose you have any way to prove you're from another planet — other than your spaceship — which for all I know could be some high-tech drug smuggling jet plane."

The stranger thought for a moment.

"Selrahcian DNA contains a triple helix nucleotide sequence."

I nodded, slow deliberate nods. "O—kay —,"

"Human DNA has a double helical structure," he added.

"I see — anything we won't need blood tests or lab work to verify?" I countered, suddenly recalling the "D" I got in high school biology.

The stranger looked down and kicked sand with his toe, like a little boy who just got caught misbehaving.

"Members of my species have a small lump just above our buttocks."

I let out a half-snort, half-guffaw that sounded like a garbage disposal grinding up a fork. He looked embarrassed and I felt bad about my lack of self-control.

"You're telling me you have a tail?"

He shrugged and nodded.

"It's a vestige of our evolutionary ancestors," he said, embarrassed.

"This is what I get for playing Good Samaritan."

But I had to hand it to this bozo — at least his line was original.

"I'll take your word for that," I said, grinning. "Is that all?"

"My tongue's pink."

"Join the club."

"You don't understand. It's really, really pink. I think the exact shade is called fuchsia." He stuck out his tongue. "See?"

Sure enough, it looked like he had just finished a strawberry Popsicle. No shrinking violet, I took a step closer.

"Keep your tongue out."

The stranger stood at attention, arms at his sides, tongue out, as if he were participating in some very weird military inspection.

I carefully examined his protruding tongue but wasn't so easily convinced. Who knows? Maybe he did just finish a lifesaver or a lollipop.

"You're gonna have to do better than that."

"No fingerprints."

"Really? Give me your hand."

I carefully examined his fingertips. The stranger wasn't lying. There were no fingerprint ridges — everyone had fingerprints and they were impossible to remove (Dillinger tried it — unsuccessfully).

"Come over here," I commanded, yanking on his hand. I pulled him over to my truck, stuck his hand under the wheel well, and rubbed his fingers against the greasy wheel bearings. Then I reached inside and snatched an old receipt off the dashboard and pressed his thumb against the paper, hard. Nothing — just a flat, black silhouette of the stranger's thumb.

"My God."

"In a manner of speaking," he said, scratching his head and trying to figure out how he was gonna get the grease off his hand.

At this point, I didn't know what to think, so I pulled a rag out of my back pocket and handed it to him.

"Thanks."

"Who are you really?" I demanded.

"What's YOUR name?" he asked, ignoring my question.

"Leddie — Why are you here?" I persisted.

"It's a rather lengthy and complex story, Leddie. Right now, I'm more concerned with finding a safe place to move my starcraft before someone else stumbles across it and I've got the Air Force, FBI or worse — a nosy scout troop — to contend with."

I found myself surprisingly calm despite having just met what could very well be an extraterrestrial visitor from another planet. I've always assumed there was other life out in space. Hell, all you had to do was look at the billions of stars stretching across the sky at night. It was hard for me to believe that dinky little Earth was the only place in the entire universe with life on it.

Much to my surprise, the stranger didn't frighten me either. In fact, I felt oddly at ease. He was a little weird, but he didn't act like the stereotypical aliens depicted in all those science fiction movies — come to Earth to destroy or enslave. Actually, he seemed like an ordinary guy having car trouble.

"My brother-in-law and I own a junkyard," I said, pointing to the orange and white patch on the navy blue coveralls I always wore to work. "Salvage Specialists." To protect myself, I made sure to mention my brother-in-law just in case this guy — alien or not — had any ulterior motives.

"Is your brother-in-law the type who might be inclined to come after me with a shotgun?"

I let out another garbage disposal half-snort. "Are you kidding? He used to be in a rock band in the sixties. He took so many acid trips back then, he'll probably recognize you."

The stranger looked both relieved and perplexed at the same time.

"Let's get back to the junkyard," I said, heading over to the truck. "We're gonna need the flatbed wrecker."

He followed and held the door open for me. I slid in behind the steering wheel, and gaped at him.

"Boy, you sure are from another planet."

He strolled around the front of the truck and climbed in the passenger side. I cranked the ignition and, with a scrunch of tires in sand, we headed back to the highway.

"So, Ithran Neg—." I didn't even want to attempt the weird name I had only heard once.

"Nek-Hånån," he said, completing his name for me — (The little dots over the "a"s are silent — I found that out later.)

"How about I just call you — ah — Nick?"

"Nick, huh?" "Nick," he repeated the name, trying it out. "Sounds good to me — and its a lot better than my given name. Ithran's a pretty dorky name even back home — the Selrahcian equivalent to Arthur or Julius."

I smiled, jammed my Jimmy into second gear, barreled over the highway shoulder and hung a right back onto State Road 256-A.

"You still haven't answered my question. What are you doing here?"

"It's my job."

"GOD has a job working for someone else?"

"I work for the Galactic Association of Star Systems."

"Galactic Association of Star — Systems?"

"It's an organization of planets formed thousands of years ago — like an interstellar United Nations, consisting of hundreds of inhabited worlds from different parts of the galaxy."

"I hope it's more effective than the U.N."

"I can vouch for the Association. It's a very efficient institution."

"And what do you do for the Association?"

"I'm a Problem Planet Administrator."

"Problem Planet Administrator?" I said, not trying to hide the trace of annoyance in my tone. He may be an okay guy, even for an alien, but he was just a little too smug to suit me. "And is Earth considered a problem?"

He gave me a sheepish grin.

"Well, yes."

I decided it was time to assume the role of self-appointed representative for the human race and continued to barrage him with questions.

"Exactly why is Earth considered a problem and what are you supposed to be doing as our administrator — or should I say — our deity?" I didn't take Baptist Bible study as a kid for nothing.

Nick paused, considered his answer, then spoke.

"Galactically speaking, problem planets generally fall into three basic categories," he replied, as if giving this dissertation was part of his job description.

"First, there are the environmentally impaired worlds. They have experienced, or are experiencing, some type of natural catastrophe or ecological crisis. The Association provides relief programs much like disaster aid here on Earth."

"Okay, that sounds reasonable."

"Next, there are the financially unstable planets. The global economy is weak or faltering and requires monetary or trade assistance."

"Sounds like we qualify under both categories."

"First things first," he said. Then he hesitated. I glared at him. "What?"

"The final classification pertains to worlds such as Earth where the so-called dominant species isn't considered advanced enough for interstellar contact. In these cases, I'm supposed to monitor the social and intellectual evolution of the species in question until such time as it progresses to the point where the Association deems it eligible for membership."

I arched my eyebrow and continued to drive without responding. The more I thought about it, the madder I got. I squinted at him just like Clint Eastwood does before some sleezeball gets blown away. It had the desired effect.

"Okay, okay," Nick said defensively. "Higher forms of sentient life have advanced technologically to the point where a self-generating, non-polluting form of energy has been developed."

"Like fusion."

"More accurately, cold fusion."

"Okay — I'll buy that."

"If the Association were to make contact with the human race before it was ready, within a few decades your pollution would have this entire star system smelling like the Nuclear Slag Pits on Erroneous II or — Bayonne, New Jersey."

Pee-uckers! I remembered driving past all those oil refineries in Bayonne on my way to New York City a few years ago. Boy, did it stink! It smelled like a kitty litter convention.

"Next —," the alien continued.

"There's more? Oh, boy!"

"Higher species have advanced to the point where they no longer commit violent crimes against each other for reasons like hatred, power, sex, money or territory."

My shoulders slumped.

"Interstellar species have recognized the counterproductive nature of such behavior." Nick shifted in his seat and draped his arm out the window. "Consider all the time, effort and money spent here on Earth trying to prevent crime, solve crimes, adjudicate and punish criminals. You'd have to agree it's an extraordinary waste of resources which could be utilized in more productive endeavors."

I leaned on the gas pedal and just stared straight ahead at the road.

"Besides, you have to have some grave reservations about members of a species who could kill one another over something as inconsequential as a soccer match."

My eyes were now trying to bore two little holes through the windshield. After a while, I curtly asked him if there was anything else.

"Your tabloid television programs are a dead giveaway that humans need more work on their social evolution."

I thought about the dregs of society that appeared on those shows — not exactly humanity at its best.
"I'll have to give you that one."

I down-shifted and turned off the highway onto the gravel driveway in front of the orange concrete block building with the large blue and white sign on top that identified it as: "Salvage Specialists—Used Auto Parts." (You were already away at school when we moved the business from the little dirt lot on Dixie Highway to this new and improved location.) Behind the building, an eight-foot-high chain link fence surrounded six acres of wrecked automobiles.

"Here we are," I announced, shutting off the engine. "It's not much, but it's mine and it pays the bills."

I paused before getting out of the truck, realizing he hadn't given me an answer to my original question. I pulled the keys from the ignition, sat back and stared at him.

"So, where does all this GOD stuff fit in?"

Chapter 5

WELL, NICK? OR should I call you your holiness or something?"

He didn't reply, but his eyes stared past my glare at something behind me.

"Hello there, Leddie," your Dad chirped with his heavy English accent. I nearly went through the roof of the truck.

"Dammit Cheeky — you scared me!"

"Sorry about that, Luv — didn't mean to." He eyed Nick. "Who's your friend?" he asked, making an exaggerated display of checking his watch and noting the time: first thing in the morning.

Nick and I climbed out of the truck. I jerked my door open quickly so that your Dad had to jump out of the way. It was my retribution for his non-verbal innuendo. His hair was still cut in the godawful Beatle mop-top and gray streaks were just starting to appear. The amount of high-octane living he had done in his earlier years was beginning to show in the craggy features of his face. Our dark blue company coveralls hung loosely on his lanky frame, making him look (at least to me) like a cross between Ichabod Crane and Herman of Herman's Hermits.

"This is Nick," I said, throwing my door shut. "Nick, this is my brother-in-law."

"Clarence H. Baztodd — but everybody calls me Cheeky." He stuck out his hand and gave Nick a hardy handshake.

"Nice to meet you."

"We need to get Nick's — ah — vehicle. It broke down east of here on 256-A — well, near 256-A. I ran across him on my way in."

"No problem. We can head out now if you like."

"You're gonna need to take the big flat bed."

"What kind of car is it?"

I hesitated, unsure of how to answer, and turned to Nick.

"He's gonna find out as soon as he sees the starship anyway," Nick said with a shrug.

"Star—ship?"

We nodded.

"Nick claims to be from a planet in another part of the galaxy. It's his starship — not his car — that crashed out there."

From the calm, almost serene expression on Cheeky's face, you would have thought we had told him Nick was a plumber or school-teacher or some other everyday occupation. He pulled a grimy rag out of his back pocket and rubbed his greasy hands.

"Another part of the galaxy, eh? Well, this'll spice up the old workweek."

Nick and I just stood there looking sheepish.

Cheeky chuckled.

"How did you convince the most skeptical person I know – who also happens to be my sister-in-law — of that?"

Nick proceeded to explain the physiological differences between his species and humans, stuck out his tongue and showed him his fingertips.

"Well, I'll bloody be! No need to show me your bum guv," Cheeky added quickly. "I'll take your word for that."

"Nick can fill you in on all the gory details later," I said.

Suddenly, from an unspecified location, a very large male Himalayan cat leaped up onto the SUV's hood, landing with a resounding fifteen pound THUD. He was a big, gorgeous caramel-colored ball of fluff with beautiful blue marble eyes, four dark brown bear paws, and a big black tail.

"Hi, handsome! How're you doing this morning?"

The big kitty purred loudly as he slinked his body under my caresses, ending with a flick of his tail as my hand reached his fluffy buttocks. I gave his butt a couple of love taps for good meas-ure.

The cat turned and looked at Nick.

How's it going? he relayed telepathically. *I'm Marlowe.*

"Well, Marlowe, it's a pleasure to meet you."

At the same instant, Cheeky and I realized Nick had no way of knowing our cat's name. We gaped at each other and then at the alien.

"How did you know Marlowe's name?" I asked.

"We're able to communicate via ultra-high frequency brain waves," he casually explained, "much higher frequencies than humans are able to receive. Many highly intelligent life forms throughout the galaxy communicate telepathically."

Highly intelligent and incredibly beautiful life forms, Marlowe added with a slow blink of his blue eyes.

You probably remember Marlowe. He was a remarkably beautiful male cat whose mellow and friendly disposition made him everybody's favorite. He knew he was everybody's favorite and wouldn't have it any other way.

I stared at my kitty as he sat on the truck hood with a self-satisfied smirk on his puss. The big stinker!

"Furthermore, felines understand every word humans say."

"What?" The weird revelations were coming much too fast and all at once. And to top it all off, it was first thing in the morning. I started trudging toward the sanctuary of my office and the happy prospect of some coffee — yes, coffee — all the while shaking my head in disbelief.

This was proving to be a most atypical day.

"Did you get the '307 pulled out of that Camaro for K&K auto?" I asked Cheeky without bothering to look back over my shoulder.

"I sure did."

"Well then, you two need to get going." I just kept on trudging.

Marlowe sauntered across the truck hood over to Nick.

Can I go too?

"Cheeky, is it alright if Marlowe comes with us?"

"Okay by me. I'll go get the wrecker and pull it around front and pick you guys up."

Marlowe sat on his abundant hindquarters and purred fast and furious.

Thanks. Mama never takes me anywhere — except to the stupid vet!

"Glad to have you along," Nick said, stroking the incredibly soft white fur under Marlowe's chin.

So, you're from another planet, eh?

"That's right."

How many inhabited worlds would you say you've visited?

"Hundreds."

In your estimation, which one has the best seafood?

Before Nick could hazard a guess, the flat-bed wrecker screeched to a halt in front of them. It was big and blue and white with a long steel car carrier on the back. Nick jerked the passenger side door open and Marlowe bounced up into the truck cab and slid in beside Cheeky. Nick was right behind him.

"You know where you ditched?"

"Yep, I crashed about thirteen miles east of here."

"Any chance the Air Force tracked your flight?" Cheeky asked, envisioning a platoon of armed National Guardsmen cordoning off the crash site.

"Not a chance," Nick said. "Most commercial starcraft are equipped with a sensory refraction system which makes them undetectable to Earth's scanning technology."

"Too bloody cool, mate."

Cheeky jammed the big truck into gear and they roared out of the driveway, the tires squealing loudly on the gravel. Marlowe craned his neck forward and peered out the windshield. He was having a ball.

"So, Cheeky, how did you get down here from southside of London?"

"You've got quite an ear for accents."

"You could say that."

"I used to be in a pop band back in the sixties. Had a pretty good run of it, too — for a couple of years anyway. Called ourselves the Peppermint Microbus. Ever hear of us?"

"Sorry."

"I guess you could say we came ashore as part of the second wave of the British rock invasion."

Marlowe made a grumpy face.

Don't get him started on all that pop music stuff. We'll never hear the end of it. Nick glanced at Marlowe but didn't say anything.

"I played guitar and sang backup — wrote most of the songs too," he said proudly. "My tune: 'Love, Love, Love Ya Luv' made it all the way to number eleven on the charts."

I told you so, Marlowe relayed.

"Our band toured with the Rascals and Little Richard."

"No kidding." Nick looked out the window. He'd feel a lot better after they retrieved his ship. "I spent some time on Earth back then," he said. "Met a pretty fine guitar player by the name of Chuck Berry. You know him?"

"Are you kidding? He's the bloody man! Met him when we played Atlanta in '69." Cheeky shifted gears and leaned on the gas. "Ole Chuck closed the show and had everyone up on their feet dancing and singing — really showed us how it's done." They were now clipping along at seventy miles an hour. "I met Leddie and Angela, Leddie's sister, after that gig."

I've heard this stupid story a million times," Marlowe relayed.

"They came up for the show and me and me band mates spotted them in a Shoney's at three in the morning."

The big kitty made a pickle puss and started mimicking everything Cheeky said.

They came up for the show and me and me band mates spotted them in a Shoney's at three in the morning. Nick covered his mouth with his hand and stifled a laugh.

"For me and Angela, it was luv at first sight." Cheeky passed a slow moving car and continued to ramble on without missing a backbeat. "We kept in touch — writing letters and running up the phone bill. After the band folded a few years later — when the bloody disco era ruined everything — I moved down here and we got married."

Bored, Marlowe nudged Nick with his snout.

You got anything to eat? I'm starving!

Marlowe was always, I mean always, hungry. Nick shrugged and shook his head.

You came halfway across the galaxy and you didn't think to bring a tuna sandwich?

Fortunately for Nick, they were nearing the crash site.

"Cheeky," he said, pointing out the window, "my ship's over there on the left, near those two large palm trees."

"Got it."

Cheeky hit the brakes, rolled to a stop and waited patiently for an oncoming old Chrysler, driven by a four foot tall, 102 year old woman, to pass. She was doing about nine and a half miles an hour. He then veered off the road and proceeded to give the wrecker's shock absorbers a high impact aerobic workout on the sandy terrain.

Marlowe had to dig his claws into the vinyl seat to keep from sliding off.

Hey — slow down! You're mussing my fluff!

As they approached the crash site, two unsteady male figures came into view. The smaller of the two men was leaning against the hull of the craft drinking a Bud tallboy. Clasped in his other hand were two unopened beers dangling by the plastic six-pack ring.

His companion stalked around the disabled ship like a tipsy aviation inspector dispatched by the nearest bar and grille to investigate the crash. He was also drinking a tallboy while his two remaining beers swayed at his side. The two men seemed to be running neck and neck in this morning's Budbowl.

The larger man was about forty, his drinking buddy in his mid-twenties. By the look of the butt cracks peering over the backsides of their dirty jeans, they appeared to be laborers of some kind. Given the day and the time of day, they were most likely unemployed laborers.

"Holey Moley!" Nick cried upon spotting the uninvited guests.

Marlowe and Cheeky gaped at each other. Holy Mo—ley?

"Drinking beer at nine o'clock in the morning?" Nick asked, genuinely surprised.

Cheeky smirked, amused by the alien's naiveté. "What are we gonna do about these guys, guv?"

Marlowe perked up.

These two bozos should be easy to get rid of. Tell them you're from NASA – no, better yet – the National Security Council. That's not as obvious. That'll get them thinking. And by the looks of them, thinking probably gives them a headache.

Nick chuckled.

"Marlowe, you're invaluable."

No kidding. I'm a feline.

"What's going on?" Cheeky asked. "What are we gonna do?"

"Just follow my lead. Back the truck up right next to the ship."

Cheeky swung the wrecker to the right, shifted into reverse, and gunned the gas.

The two interlopers had to stumble over each other to get out of the way, but they never relinquished control of their brews

Cheeky cut the engine and he and Nick climbed out of the cab while Marlowe stayed perched on the front seat and peered over the top of the dashboard.

"How are you gentlemen today?" Nick said, as politely as possible.

"You guys come to get this thing?" the smaller man asked.

"That's correct," Cheeky replied.

"This some kinda Stealth Bomber or something?" the taller and older of the two asked with a belch and a guffaw. He acted like he had just come up with the greatest line in comedy history.

The little one laughed and poked his buddy in the ribs with his elbow.

"Stealth Bomber. Biff, you're one funny sumbitch."

"That's exactly what it is," Nick said with authority. "Experimental military aircraft, state of the art and, of course, top secret."

The two drunks stopped laughing.

"Who the hell are you?" Biff demanded.

"I'm Nick, ah — Adams, N-S-C."

"What's that?"

"National Security Council, sir."

Biff and his pal eyed Nick's Key West T-shirt and Cheeky's coveralls. Something wasn't adding up.

"That's right," Cheeky said, trying his best to sound like Sean Connery. "We've been sent — undercover — to retrieve this, ah — classified aircraft."

Biff belched again, this time in Cheeky's direction.

"And who are you supposed to be — James Fuckin' Bond?"

More hysterics from the smaller man.

"Actually, I AM with the Double-0 Section," Cheeky replied. "Licensed to KILL," he added ominously. "And who might you be?"

"I'm Biff Breeto and this is my little brother, Chili," the bigger man replied, as if their names were actually of some significance.

Nick stepped past the inebriates, his face grim.

"I'm gonna have to ask you both, in the interest of national security, to keep anything and everything you've seen here to yourselves," he said, officiously examining the starcraft.

In unison, Biff and his brother tossed their spent tallboys away, pulled fresh ones and popped the tops. For Biff, the wheels inside his head were perpetrating a DUI.

"What the hell do we get out of it?" he grunted.

"The satisfaction that you're doing your country a service," Nick replied. It was more of a question than an answer.

The tall drunk wiped his mouth with the back of his hand and mulled Nick's response over for a second.

"No way. Come on, Chili, let's go talk to our cousin's uncle's stepsister."

Nick and Cheeky glanced at each other and unsuccessfully tried to ascertain the convoluted family connection.

"She's with the Sheriff's Department," Biff informed them. "We're gonna tell her everything we've seen here."

"Yeah, we're gonna tell her all about this here jetplane and get ourselves on 'Inside Edition,' Little Chili announced, bolstered by his brother's bravado.

Biff turned toward his companion. "Yeah, or 'Extra'."

"Yeah, I wonder if we'll get to meet Mary Hart?" Chili asked, meandering off the track slightly.

"That's 'Entertainment Tonight,' stupid," Biff snapped. "Come on. Let's go. See you guys on the news."

They stormed off in the opposite direction of the highway.

"Think they're a problem?" Cheeky asked.

"Who would believe them?"

Cheeky nodded and then called out to Biff and Chili.

"Hey, you blokes, happy hour just started over at Brewski's Pub."

The revelers stopped in their tracks, held up their plastic rings and realized they were down to their last beer each. They continued on their way after performing a slight course correction.

"What do you say we get your ship back to the junkyard, guv?"

Chapter
6

THE MAIN BUILDING at Salvage Specialists — the "showroom" as I used to jokingly call it — was a former single-story, 2 bedroom, $1\frac{1}{2}$ bath, concrete block Florida house built in the 1940's. The renovations converting it to commercial use included removal of the wall dividing the living and dining areas and the addition of two steel garage doors, one on each side that led out to the back lot. During the workweek, these doors were left up to allow customers, who wanted to pull their own parts, easy access to the hundreds of wrecked cars in the yard.

A long, waist-high wooden counter, covered with fake mahogany wood paneling, divided the showroom in half. With the exception of about a two square foot area directly over the cash drawer — the rest of the countertop was covered with stray distributor caps, pistons, wheel bearings and windshield wipers from every make and model of car in automotive history. There were door panels and hubcaps lining the walls, wheel drums and crankshafts stacked in every corner. (Needless to say, I'm not the most organized person when it comes to inventory storage.)

An old battery and a driveshaft held open double doors behind the counter that led to two small bedrooms that were converted into my office and a repair bay equipped with a hydraulic lift.

Against the wall opposite the counter, we built a big stone fireplace with an oak mantle and a slate hearth (mainly because during the winter it was always so cold in there). Like the rest of the showroom, there were clutches, sideview mirrors and voltage regulators lining the mantle and hearth and a flywheel assembly resting in the fireplace. (I usually tried to firesale — no pun intended — anything in there before the weather turned cold.)

Cheeky pulled the front seat out of a '67 Cadillac, shoved against the wall next to the fireplace and that served as the Salvage Specialists' customer lounge (pretty plush).

It was nearing noon on the day I found Nick and his ship, and I was manning the counter. Opposite me stood a wiry young man wearing jeans and a grease-stained Allman Brothers Band T-shirt. A freshly lit Marlboro hung out of one side of his mouth.

Nick, Cheeky and Marlowe appeared in the doorway.

Marlowe immediately trotted across the room and bounced up to one of his favorite spots on the fireplace hearth. He rested his big butt against an '01 Cougar fuel pump and hunkered down for a nap.

"If we pull it," I told the customer, "it'll be an extra ten bucks." I turned my attention away from the customer to the duo at the door. "Don't you two go anywhere!" I yelled, with a stomp of my foot.

Nick and Cheeky immediately plopped down on the Cadillac seat. I think I scared them. The customer glanced back over his shoulder at them and then started to dig some money out of his pocket.

"No, I'll pull it myself," the young man said, his cigarette butt bobbing up and down in the corner of his mouth.

"Okay, that'll be thirty-four fifty."

Cheeky poked Nick in the side with his elbow.

"Watch Leddie. This is amazing!"

"Ow!" Nick whined, rubbing where Cheeky's bony elbow had jabbed him.

The customer forked over two crumpled-up tens and a twenty, and I handed him his change and a receipt.

"There's a gray '82 Malibu Classic, with a smashed rear end. It's six rows back on the left about halfway down the row. The alternator out of that Malibu will fit your Nova."

Cheeky smirked.

"We don't need a computer to keep track of our inventory. Leddie's got a bloody 50,000 megabyte system right there in her noggin. Six acres of wrecked cars and she knows exactly where each and every salvageable part is and can recall its location faster than a microchip-gobbling alternating current."

He was always bragging about my ability to keep our inventory straight in my head.

The young man departed with a nod and a "thanks."

"It's incredible how she keeps all that information stored in her brain," Cheeky continued. "And, I might add, besides being my wife's kid sister, she's a wonderful person."

"Where the hell have you two been all morning?" I snarled. "I need that exhaust manifold pulled for Mahoney's."

"We retrieved Nick's ship."

"Yeah."

"And put it in the utility shed."

"Okay."

"But first we had to clean out the shed."

"Alright."

"There was a bloody awful mess in there."

"Yeah."

"Mostly useless junk – tons of it."

"Uh-huh." I tried not to show it, but Cheeky was wearing me down.

"And we put the ship in there and I got Nick some tools, and,"

"Okay, okay!" I huffed and puffed. "The guy from Mahoney's is coming by at one."

"Gotcha covered Luv."

Cheeky bolted up to his feet and retreated. "See ya' later, Nick."

Safe in the knowledge that your Dad was on his way to pull the required exhaust manifold, my frustration quickly subsided.

Nick stood up and inched over to the counter.

"Leddie, I just wanted to thank you for everything you've done for me. And I want you to know I'm gonna try my best to fix the ship and be on my way as soon as possible."

"Oh. Hey, no problem. I mean, how often do we get visitors from another planet?" I placed the customer's change in the cash drawer and bumped it shut with my hip. "Besides, you can help Cheeky to earn your keep and pay for a new paint job for my truck roof."

"Can I build a solar panel?" he asked.

"A solar panel? That sounded expensive. "Can you use stuff from the yard to build it?"

"I think so."

"Knock yourself out."

"Thanks Leddie – thanks a lot!"

Then he stared at me with a strange grin on his face. Later, when I looked in the mirror, I found grease smudges on my chin and left cheek. Some great interplanetary impression I must've made.

He turned to leave.

"After work, Cheeky and I are gonna order pizza and get some beer," I said. "Do you eat — ah — human food?"

"Pizza! Geeze Louise — I love pizza!"

"Great. I'll order some just before we close for the day."

Smiling, Nick headed out the door.

I shook my head. "Geeze — Louise?"

— — —

Nick entered the large, steel-roofed utility shed and immediately went to work. Before he attempted to test the ship's systems, he needed to determine if the primary power grid near the bottom of the fuselage was damaged in the crash. He pulled a socket wrench out of the tool box Cheeky had provided, knelt down on his hands and knees on the dirt floor and began to unscrew the grid's retaining bolts. With his attention focused on the task at hand, he didn't notice the slender female Russian Blue cat slink into the shed until they were nose to nose.

Her emerald eyes flashed.

Who are you?

There was a military camouflage kerchief knotted around her neck and she wore two small ammunition belts across her chest, Mexican bandito style. She possessed the air of a tiny jungle lioness returning from the hunt.

"I'm Nick from Selrahc."

The feline brain waves bore into his cranium.

Where's that?

"It's about 200 light years past the constellation you call Taurus."

Oh. The gray cat relaxed ever so slightly. Nick's response seemed to be acceptable to his new acquaintance and he exhaled, feeling like he had passed some type of initiation.

I'm Sergeant Nikki – perimeter patrol. I protect the junkyard perimeter against usurpers, she relayed.

From what Nick could determine, her brain wave patterns were transmitting in a perfectly logical manner.

"Great. It's nice to meet you Nikki."

She scowled at Nick for what seemed like an hour but was, in fact, only a few seconds, and then turned and started to saunter out of the shed.

I'll be in touch alien.

Nick sat in the dirt and considered the strange little creature. And he thought the Rain Forests on Ohilibama IV contained some weird species!

I heard that — Selrahc.

After a few moments of sitting in stupefied silence, Nick went back to work. He found the power grid unaffected by the crash and, considering the tumble the starcraft took, this stroke of luck was nothing short of miraculous.

With the exception of the failed lift stabilizer and hundreds of dings and dents sustained in the crash, everything else seemed to be in satisfactory condition. He would have to recharge the reactor activation cells to get the ship's fusion core operational, but that would require the construction of a solar panel and some time.

He reached in the cockpit and switched on the primary power systems. The Bablona 66-L, which was located next to the co-pilot's chair, lit up.

Physically, the computer resembled an oversized Marantz 22 Series stereo tuner. Black and silver metal framed a front panel of blue lights. There was a red power lamp on the left, and a white voice indicator in the center that flashed when the computer spoke.

"Downtime was three hours, seven minutes and nine seconds," Babs stated immediately upon activation.

"It's great to have you back on line, Babs."

"We are not at the same location coordinates," she reported.

"No, we're at a junkyard called Salvage Specialists."

"12.851 kilometers west southwest of our previous position."

"That's correct. Please perform a full system analysis. I'm gonna look through the junkyard for some parts to build a solar panel."

"Affirmative. The reactor activation cells require recharging."

Nick started for the door of the shed.

The voice indicator lamp flashed once more.

"Please define: junkyard."

———   ———   ———

Nick spent the rest of the day rummaging through the six acres of wrecked autos looking for enough recycled parts to jury-rig a solar panel. It was about five-thirty when I entered the shed and heard him tinkering with something inside the spacecraft and conversing with — someone?

"Excellent, Bablona."

"Who are you talking to?" I asked, stepping in and glancing around the interior of the shed.

"Hello, Leddie. This is Bablona 66-L, the ship's computer," Nick said, pointing inside the cockpit at the electronic face of blue light.

I edged over to the ship and peeked in the open hatch.

"Do I just say hello?"

"Of course."

"It is a pleasure to meet you, Leddie," Babs announced.

"Wow, she really does sound like me. Ah, nice to meet you, too." I felt a little weird talking to a machine.

"Nick, do you mind if I take a look?" I asked, motioning with my head toward the rear compartment of the ship.

"Sure, help yourself."

I hopped through the hatch, stepped past the pilot's chair and walked back into the cabin area behind the cockpit. Incredibly, it looked as big as the average two-bedroom (two bath) apartment. There were all sorts of high tech consoles lining one wall and a large viewscreen on the other. There was also a galley table that seated four and, in the aft section, what seemed like doors leading to — more rooms? For a spacecraft that looked from the outside like it wasn't much bigger than a corporate jet, it sure had a lot of square footage.

"It's so big in here," I said, wandering around.

"The spatial disorientation you are experiencing is due to the ship's IHE System," Bablona informed me.

"The what?"

"The Internal Holographic Enhancement System."

"Oh."

"It utilizes holographic projection throughout the cabin area to provide the illusion of additional space."

With her sexy voice, the computer sounded like one of those models working the auto show.

"This allows commercial starcraft passengers maximum comfort while reducing overall hull weight which is critical to achieving and maintaining ultra-light speeds."

"Wow, that's pretty cool." The wonders of galactic technology.

"Could you please explain the derivation of — Nick?"

"Huh? Oh, ah, yeah," I stammered, surprised more by the form of the question rather than the content. "That's what we call Ithran because his real name is too hard to pronounce."

"Understood and logged into data memory."

There was a pause and then the white voice lamp flashed again.

"Nick is less difficult to utilize and – to use a current Earth euphemism — less nerdy."

I started to laugh. For a computer, Bablona seemed pretty cool.

"I like her, Nick," I said, climbing out the hatch. "Come on, the pizza's here and Cheeky bought a couple of six packs."

"Pizza!" the alien exclaimed with glee. "Great, I'm starved."

After bidding Bablona goodnight, we headed out the door of the utility shed.

Chapter 7

AS WE STROLLED across the yard, Nick recalled his encounter with the strange little gray kitty.

"Who is that strange little gray cat that roams around the junk-yard?"

I couldn't help but smile and shake my head.

"I see you've met Nikki. She's Marlowe's little sister."

"I'm from another planet, hundreds of light years from here. I've traveled extensively throughout this part of the galaxy, have had contact with species from the most distant and exotic worlds known to the Association and I consider Nikki one of the strangest creatures I've ever met."

"That's our Nikki. My sister, Angela, found her in a burned out building in Kuwait during Operation Desert Storm. Angela's a Lieutenant with the 29th EVAC, First Marine Division. Nikki was only a kitten when Angela found her crouched under some rubble, cold and hungry."

"I guess that explains her — accessories," Nick said.

"You mean her — uniform."

"Yeah."

"Poor baby. Through some connections Angela had in the Quartermaster General's office, she was able to get Nikki shipped back here to us. Don't ask me how she pulled it off — but she did."

We paused to step around what appeared, in the fading daylight, to be a rusty driveshaft that was in our path.

"Cheeky says Nikki's a tripwire kitty, and constantly relives her war experiences over and over. She patrols the outskirts of the junk-yard and goes ballistic if any unfamiliar cats come near the fence – especially Persian cats."

Nick nodded thoughtfully as if this all made perfect sense to him, which, of course, it didn't.

Beer in hand, Cheeky was hunched over the showroom counter when we arrived. He had already downed one Guinness Stout and was halfway through his second. There was a plastic cooler filled with ice cold bottles of beer sitting on the floor and two open pizza boxes on the counter.

"Have a beer. There's Guinness and Budweiser."

"Budweiser's fine," Nick said.

"Grab some pizza, too. We've got pepperoni and mushroom and one with everything on it."

I grabbed a Bud longneck on my way past the cooler, sat down on a stool behind the counter and twisted the cap off. I took a long, satisfying first pull off it and then snatched a slice of pepperoni and mushroom. I allowed Nick just enough time to grab a beer, some pizza and a spot on the fireplace hearth before springing my ambush.

"I believe you were going to answer a question for me – our father who art in orbit."

Nick was busy munching away when his eyes met my expectant gaze. He swallowed hard.

"Oh, yeah, the GOD question," he groaned, sounding sorry he ever opened his big interplanetary mouth.

Cheeky took a swig of stout.

"The — God — question?" he asked, watching the alien with keen interest, and fortifying himself with another healthy jolt of Guinness.

"As I told Leddie before, when she found my ship," Nick explained for Cheeky's benefit, "I come from a planet known as Selrahc which is located on the other side of what you call the Taurus star group. I work for the Galactic Association of Star

Systems which is an interstellar organization of planets. I've been employed as an administrator for the Association's Problem Planet Department for the equivalent of four thousand Earth years."

Cheeky choked on his beer.

"Four thousand years!"

"Geeze Louise!" I gulped, then caught myself. "Geeze — Louise. Now you've got me doing it, Nick."

"Just how old are you?" Cheeky asked.

"It's difficult to compare my age in terms of 365-day years."

"How come?"

"Well, first of all — as what is known on Earth as Einstein's Theory of Relativity correctly postulates, time slows down drastically for objects moving at very high speeds. The faster my starship travels, for example, the slower time passes for me. Galactic employees with interstellar responsibilities — like mine — spend a lot of time traveling at faster-than-light speeds. Because of this, we don't age like the planet-bound."

Nick paused to chomp some more pizza and sip his beer.

"In fact, I knew a young star freighter pilot who had a taste for Moogalian Emerald Ale. He spent so much time traveling through space at ultra-light speeds that, when he returned to Moogalie after an extended voyage, he was actually younger than when he left and, unfortunately for him, under the planet's legal drinking age."

"Bloody unbelievable."

Marlowe, who had been napping on the fireplace mantle, awoke from a sound sleep and sat up.

Do I smell anchovies?

"Secondly, many species from other parts of the galaxy have life spans much longer than humans. Because of their physiological makeup, some beings live for centuries."

"Centuries?" I said, glancing over at Cheeky. We don't even get a whole one of those."

"Betcha most of these old beings end up retiring to Florida," Cheeky joked.

"Most galactic personnel are chosen from species that live very long lives relative to humans," Nick added.

"Why is that?" I asked.

"Primarily due to the fact that, galactically speaking, all the star systems that support intelligent, sentient life are so unbelievably far away from each other. It takes incredible amounts of time to traverse the known reaches of the galaxy."

Cheeky and I nodded and sipped more beer.

"Take Earth, for example," he continued. "On a galactic scale, your planet is like the Amazon tribes inhabiting the deepest part of the rain forest. Because they live in such remote and hard to reach locations, very few outsiders have had contact with them. Earth is as remote, but the distances cover thousands of light years instead of miles."

Marlowe had been listening to the conversation from his perch atop the fireplace mantle. He hopped down onto the hearth next to Nick's stool and sat ramrod straight, his proud feline profile a testament to his ability to grasp the intellectual and scientific concepts being discussed.

You gonna eat those anchovies, Nick?

"No, you can have them, Marlowe." Nick pulled two of the salty fishes off his pizza slice and set them down on the floor.

Thanks! Marlowe relayed, devouring the anchovies in two quick gulps.

"I read somewhere that the nearest star to our solar system is so far away that it would take four years to reach traveling at the speed of light," Cheeky said in-between bites of a slice of pepperoni and mushroom.

"That's where the wormholes come in," Nick said, turning his attention back to our discussion.

"Wormholes?" we humans cried in unison.

"Wormholes are tunnels of contorted space-time that can traverse thousands — sometimes millions of light years in relatively short periods of time and emerge in different areas of the galaxy. They're subspace pathways, so to speak, through the space-time continuum."

Nick noticed our blank stares.

I understand. Marlowe was the only one present to respond, although he was more interested in Nick's pizza toppings.

"A wormhole is like an interstellar Panama Canal connecting two huge oceans of galactic space. Instead of sailing all the way around South America, you just slip through the subspace canal." We sat in silence trying to digest our pizza, beer and Nick's astounding revelations (not necessarily in that order).

"One wormhole, for example, begins about five light years from a planet called Baltrus VII and ends just outside Pluto near your solar system. That's a distance of just over forty-five hundred light years."

"Bloody well hope it's not a toll road," Cheeky quipped.

"This is all very interesting, but it still doesn't explain your GOD comment," I said, growing impatient.

"Judas Priest," Nick said with resignation. He picked a pepperoni off his pizza wedge and gave it to Marlowe.

"Okay — here goes," he gulped. "Due to unexpected operational difficulties with my starcraft, I've been forced to spend an inordinate amount of time here on Earth. During these unscheduled and sometimes extended stays, I have formulated a conclusion about the human race."

"And what's that?" Cheeky asked a half-second before I did.

"Humans take themselves and their place in the universe far too seriously."

"Oh, really," I said with the disdain I reserved for Nick's special brand of interplanetary egotism. It was becoming annoying.

"Humans assume they are the most intelligent and highly advanced species on Earth because they build strip malls and ICBM's and watch cable television." The alien paused to sip some brew. "But you're not."

"Then who is the most advanced species?" I tried to sound like a homicide detective grilling a murder suspect.

"In descending order: dolphins, whales, cats, human females, human males."

Cheeky thumped his beer bottle down on the countertop.

"That's the biggest bloody crock of kitty litter I've ever heard."

Nick was unfazed by his stout-induced bluster.

"Consider this. Humans spend, on the average, fifty weeks a year slaving away at their jobs just to earn enough money to pay their bills and take off for two weeks to swim in the ocean on vacation."

"Yeah — so?" I challenged the alien.

"For dolphins, swimming in the ocean IS their job! Are you gonna tell me humans are more intelligent?"

"They do have bigger brains than us," Cheeky conceded. "And, they communicate with each other about ten times faster than we talk."

"Don't encourage him," I snapped.

"In fact, if it wasn't for humans, Earth would probably have been accepted into the Association years ago."

I always suspected that humans held us felines back from realizing our true potential.

"And cats?" I asked, glancing warily over at Marlowe.

Be kind, Nick, they're only humans.

"Same thing; you don't see members of the feline species slogging off to work forty hours a week and then panicking when they realize they've come home without human food."

How undignified, Marlowe relayed for Nick's benefit.

"But their brains are so much smaller than ours," Cheeky pointed out.

"That's true, but they use ALL of their brain capacity. Unlike some species around here who only utilize about five percent of their total brain mass."

Cheeky and I slouched on our stools. Unfortunately, I remembered reading something about that in a magazine.

"This superior attitude is inconsistent with the way advanced life forms think and has stunted the intellectual and social development of the human race. Over the last few thousand years, I've tried to — ah — assist your species along the appropriate evolutionary path, thus allowing your planet to — "

"No longer be considered a problem?" I was getting pissed.

"Yes, exactly." Nick's tone had changed from condescending to defensive.

"What kind of help are you talking about, mate?" Cheeky asked after polishing off his second stout, and pulling another one out of the cooler.

Nick gulped again.

"Do you remember the Bible story concerning Moses and the parting of the Red Sea?"

Cheeky and I exchanged quick worried glances.

"Moses was leading the tribe of Israel out of captivity with the Egyptians hot on their trail. They made it to the shore of the Red Sea which blocked their escape."

"Yeah?" I said, trying to hide the apprehension in my voice.

"By flying low over the water, the fusion thrusters of my starcraft made a nice wide part in the sea and allowed them to cross to safety."

Our respective gasts flabbered; Cheeky and I chugged some beer.

"Really quite simple," Nick said, very proud of himself.

Cheeky, feeling the effects of the Guinness, grunted.

"What're you gonna tell us next, mate? You sent Jesus Bloody Christ, too?"

"His real name was GonFolan and he was a philosophy professor and holistic healer from Geren IV."

"That takes care of the Jews and the Christians," I shot back. "Don't tell me you forgot about the Muslims and the Buddhists?"

"Ruma Iamim from Xylos IX and Buddha — we didn't have to change his name — from Perxis XII."

Nick gnawed on his pizza crust as we were, once again, rendered speechless.

"I had high hopes that their teachings and example would bring about peace and understanding to the people of this world. Unfortunately, as well-intentioned as my motives were, their messages were soon perverted and used throughout Earth's history for political and financial gain and to justify violence and bigotry against others."

Sadly, we had no defense for Nick's accusations but my mind was racing.

"What would possess you to interfere with our planet in the first place?" I charged. "After all, we're such lowly, insignificant creatures."

Nick squirmed and chugged his beer.

"I don't know," he said after another hard swallow. "The human race, although underdeveloped, has many endearing qualities and vast potential."

"Like Rock and Roll," Cheeky said.

"Can you elaborate?" I said, ignoring your Dad's example. He wasn't helping.

"Well, your species seems to grow from a crisis or challenge — especially when the status quo's been upset. Humans perform above their talents and resources to retrieve what's been lost or taken from them."

"Like Britain and the Allies kicking Hitler's arse in World War II," Cheeky said with pride.

"Yes, exactly. The capacity to accomplish extraordinary feats and endure unimaginable hardships seems to dissipate once the status quo's been reestablished and complacency sets in."

"So?" I said. I know, pretty lame — but it was the best I could do in the heat of the moment.

"Imagine what the human race could accomplish if this same capacity for greatness were a way of life?"

"We'd probably all have bloody heart attacks before we're thirty."

"But is it wise to interfere in matters that will affect an entire planet and millions of people?" I flung my crust into the open pizza box. "Is it wise to PLAY GOD?"

This time — Mister Advanced Galactic Being, interstellar traveler and representative of the Galactic Association of Star Systems — had no answer. All he could do was hang his head like a recalcitrant schoolboy caught smoking in the boy's room.

Chapter
8

Enforcement Department Assistant First Class Antage Lotan marched toward the space dock conveniently located adjacent to the Regional Galactic Complex on Baltrus VII.

It was another day of absolutely perfect weather on the planet — the suns were shining and the cobalt blue sky cloudless. Diverse beings from all corners of the known galaxy strolled the grounds (if they were bipedal life forms) conversing and enjoying the warm sunshine. It was impossible to be in foul spirits on such a beautiful day.

Antage Lotan was in a baaa—d mood.

With a scowl on his face that told everyone within sensor range to "back off," he hopped on the being mover and continued to chugg along on the slow, but steady, moving conveyor.

Impatiently awaiting his arrival next to their departmental starcraft was Lotan's partner, Enforcement Assistant Third Class, Avith Skairac.

Both were natives of Nebo-Jaasu II, a planet whose race of intelligent humanoids were built like NFL linebackers. Nebo men and women were famous for their physical prowess and consistently outperformed opponents in the Pan Galactic Games held every four hundred years on Uhhicihcus III.

Throughout galactic society, violent crime was extremely rare and civil authorities were — well — civil. Even so, being built like very large football players did nothing to hinder Antage and Avith in the effective dispatch of their Enforcement Department duties.

The planet of Nebo-Jaasu II was a world plagued with coastal erosion problems so severe that, over the last several millennia, its continents experienced the loss of over sixty percent of their original land mass. Because of this, the Nebo-Jassuians were forced to migrate further and further inland away from their ever-vanishing shorelines. They crowded into a small handful of urban population centers and lived in an environment similar to that of Earth's largest and most densely populated cities.

Crammed into massive metropolises teeming with billions of inhabitants, commuter-stuffed mass transit systems, and homicidal taxi drivers, the Nebo-Jaasuians evolved into an abrupt, caustic and cynical society that was always in a hurry.

Although not evil or malevolent by nature, the Nebos prided themselves on their toughness and made it clear to species from other worlds that it would be wise not to mess with them.

The planet's population was comparable to a world-wide society comprised exclusively of 2.6 billion New Yorkers.

It'll come as no surprise to you that the precise translation of the Nebo-Jaasuian common greeting — the equivalent to "hello" in other languages — was: "The fuck YOU looking at?"

This race of beings was perfectly suited for Enforcement Department duty.

Avith couldn't help but notice his partner's dark scowl.

"You pissed off about something?"

"Damn right I'm pissed. We've been ordered to Earth to pick up a suspect — a Capital Murder suspect."

The extremely rare violent crime of Capital Murder was certain to elicit a response nothing short of incredulity from his partner.

"Earth," he moaned. "Zadar's radar! We've got to go all the way out to that jerkwater planet? Talk about the vesicountal reflux (armpit) of the galaxy."

"Damn straight," Antage spat. "And if that weren't bad enough, the atmosphere is substandard."

Merek and Velitel, who had been tailing Antage, also hopped off the being mover at the Enforcement Department docking area. The well-connected galactic attorney had called in a favor from a certain female subspace communications dispatcher and found out that Antage and Avith were assigned to bring Nek-Hånån in to stand trial. The dispatcher stopped short of revealing their destination despite an impressive display of the lawyer's charisma.

Merek, comm-case in one hand, clutched a white paper bag in the other. Velitel carried a zero-gravity hydro thermos.

"If you can divert their attention while the vehicle hatch is open, I can scan their flight logs with my comm-unit," Merek said.

"I'll just turn on the charm."

Merek chuckled.

"I don't think our situation is THAT desperate."

The lawyer snatched the bag from his partner in crime.

"I'll have no problem getting their undivided attention," he said, holding up the bag and thermos.

They scurried over to the space-docked starcraft and Velitel flashed a congenial smile and waved a congenial wave just as Antage and Avith were about to board.

"How are you gentlemen today?"

They curtly returned the lawyer's greeting and informed him they were in a hurry and needed to get going.

"Whatta ya want?" Antage snapped.

The cynical and suspicious nature of the Nebo was not going to help the devious duo pull off their simplistic ruse.

"Where are you guys headed?" the attorney asked, all wide-eyed and innocent.

Merek, in the meantime, nonchalantly strolled up near the starship hatch and switched his comm-unit on.

"Can't tell you, Azor. That's confidential information – Regional Council business."

"I understand."

"What's it to you?" Avith said.

"Nothing," Velitel replied, "just making conversation."

Antage suddenly turned towards Merek and the large Beoran was forced to maneuver in a manner that looked something like Marlon Brando performing Swan Lake. Merek quickly feigned interest in their ship.

"Betcha this'll get you guys across the galaxy and back pretty fast," he said, mugging like an envious teenage ogling a buddy's hot rod.

"Yeah, sure, it'll do the job," a suspicious Antage said, eyeing him up and down.

Velitel jumped to his pal's rescue.

"Merek and I were planning to spend the rest of this morning enjoying a nice leisurely breakfast but we've been called before the Regional Council."

"We're definitely not looking forward to listening to Jidlaph on an empty stomach," Merek groaned, overacting just a tad.

"Yeah, tell us about it," Avith said, recalling the endless hours he had suffered listening to the Council bigmouth drone on and on.

"Anyway," the lawyer explained, "we're not gonna have time for these Olgarian Pastries or this Expresso from Maris IX. You guys interested?"

"Olgarian Pastries!"

The two Enforcement Assistants lit up like a couple of kids on the morning of the Sacred Feast of Xylos and Merek, ever so slowly, edged back over to the open hatch.

"You got some chocolate covered?" Avith asked.

Chocolate was chocolate in all parts of the known galaxy.

"There's all kinds in there, boys," Velitel said, his slow, distinctive Selrahcian drawl made the offer all the more appealing.
Antage and Avith were too busy pawing the white bag to notice Merek scanning the flight logs inside the cockpit with his comm-unit.

"Thanks, Azor," Antage said.

"You too, Merek," Avith added, without turning his attention away from the bag of goodies.

"Don't forget your coffee."

Within seconds the deceptively stealthy Merek was back next to Velitel — mission accomplished. They stood side by side, lightly bouncing up and down on the balls of their feet.

Overjoyed, the two happy Enforcement Department campers promptly boarded their ship and, with a wave out the cockpit window, fired up the fusion thrusters and slowly steered out of space dock.

Merek and Velitel smiled and waved until the craft was space-borne, and then consulted the comm-unit.

"Earth," Merek said. "They're headed for Earth."

"Let's send a subspace transmission before they break orbit and can monitor outgoing comm-signals."

Merek accessed one of his department's secured frequencies and quickly dispatched the brief coded message they had composed earlier.

"There. The transmission should reach Earth before they do."

"Great."

Merek punched a couple more buttons on his comm-unit.

"Approximately forty-nine hours before the ED ship reaches Earth orbit."

"Excellent," the lawyer said, playfully slapping his buddy on the arm. Merek looked up from his comm-unit.

"What?" he asked, trying to figure out the reason for his companion's mischievous grin.

"I saved you a pastry."

Chapter 9

IT WAS ANOTHER typical lazy Sunday afternoon at Salvage Specialists. This was primarily due to the fact that the junkyard is closed on Sundays. The sun was bright in the royal blue Florida sky and early winter temperature mild. While Nick toiled on his solar panel out near the back fence, I could be found in the utility shed sitting in the starcraft's cockpit.

"There are 5642 charted Association star systems, containing 1449 planets possessing nitrogen-hydrogen-oxygen atmospheres," Bablona 66-L stated in response to a question I had just posed. "Eight hundred and ten of these support various forms of sentient carbon-based life."

"Unbelievable," I said, idly swiveling back and forth in the co-pilot's chair.

"I believe it is my turn to ask a question of you," Babs said.

"Okay, shoot."

The computer paused.

"I do not understand your last instruction."

"Ask, Bablona, ask your question."

"Thirteen row back, fifteenth unit in, to the right."

"1967 Chevy Camaro Convertible, maroon, heavy damage to the left side," I responded within a nanosecond. "Salvageable parts: 250 cc straight six engine – rebuilt and sold, alternator; voltage regulator, right door, two front bucket seats—also sold; right rear quarter panel, front bumper, right front fender—still on the unit." I looked at my new high-tech companion and grinned. "You know,

Babs, there's no way for you to know if I'm bullshitting you about my inventory."

"Please define: 'bullshitting'."

Wow, that one blew me out the airlock and into deep space. I had to take a moment to think. Everyone knew exactly what bullshitting was until you had to try and explain it to someone — or something — that didn't.

"Well, it's not telling the truth — or exaggerating the truth."

The computer's cybernetic blue face remained silent for precisely 6.17 seconds.

"It is not productive to alter factual data."

"Oh, Babs," I said with a condescending tone. I couldn't help but smile, finding her directness refreshing. Bablona's propensity to speak in precise terms had a strangely innocent and endearing quality.

"A lot of humans think they can be — more productive — if they alter or exaggerate the truth."

"That is one reason why humans are not considered eligible for membership in the Association — one of 1161 reasons."

"Eleven hundred and sixty-one? Boy, the Association seems awful picky."

"The Association has had thirty-four point eighty-five millennia to formulate and codify its policies and procedures."

"What will it take for the human race to be accepted?"

I couldn't believe I was starting to bond with a computer system.

"That is an excellent question," Babs replied. "First, the age of the human species must be taken into consideration. Humans are an extremely young race, existing in its current state of physiological development for a mere 4.25 million years. Consequently, humans are considered an immature species. Character traits such as hatred, greed and jealousy are typical of immature species. Status as galactic beings requires evolving to the point where these types of behavior are no longer prevalent."

I felt like I was getting a lecture from my mother.

"Are you talking about evolution — like Darwin evolution?"

"In a manner of speaking. The human species must advance in their social development in order to bring about solutions to many of the social and political problems affecting your planet."

I was about to reply but Babs' white voice lamp continued to flicker without stopping. Too bad she didn't have to pause to catch her breath.

"Higher forms of sentient life have advanced beyond the predisposition towards intolerance of others based on differences in race, nationality, sexual orientation, political and religious beliefs, height, weight and preference in professional sports teams."

I was racking my brain for something to say in defense of the human race but Babs continued her dissertation.

"Most importantly, humans are unable to utilize the vast power of their own minds. Humans only use five —,"

"Yeah, yeah, I know," I interrupted. "Five percent of our brains — Nick's always itching for an opportunity to point that one out."

"The ability to utilize higher percentages of brain capacity will lead to overall sociological development."

"Like telepathy," I concluded aloud.

"That is an excellent example."

"Ooo — I'd know just what Marlowe was up to all the time — the big stinker." A sly smile appeared on my face at the thought of that prospect. "How long do you think this development will take?"

"Not very long — perhaps five or six hundred years."

"Oh," I said, disappointed.

"Always remember, Leddie, the universe is vast and limitless and you contain those same infinite qualities within your own mind."

Boy, for a computer, albeit a highly advanced interstellar computer, Bablona could come up with some pretty deep insights.

Then, from some incalculable recess of cyberspace came: "Leddie, do you have a mate?"

"Excuse me?"

Babs sounded really weird when she attempted to engage in personal discussion — kinda like a bizarre combination of Marilyn Monroe and the robot from "Lost in Space."

"I had one," I replied, "but I got rid of him."

"Why? That seems — unproductive."

"Ha, that's a laugh. Actually, he was the one who was unproductive — not to mention selfish, inconsiderate and unable to recognize my value as a person unless it was directly related to his needs — which usually involved drinking a lot of beer."

I spotted a really cool-looking, aquamarine-colored control on a panel just above my head and reached out to touch it.

"Please do not adjust the Internal Environment Sub-System."

"Sorry," I said, jerking my hand back.

"My circuitry must remain at a constant 61.9 degrees Gilibus in order to maintain optimum operational efficiency."

"Oh, sorry — anyway, at least I got the junkyard in the divorce settlement."

"How was that accomplished?"

"Salvage Specialists was a profitable business when my ex-husband inherited it from his parents, but he promptly let it go to hell in a handbasket. The judge figured nobody could do a worse job of running the place and awarded it to me. When I took over, I promptly fired my ex."

"Please define: 'hell in a handbasket'."

"Gee, I don't know — it's like when something's — malfunctioning — make that: seriously malfunctioning."

"Understood and logged into data storage."

The blue lights of Bablona's face panel stared at me for another 6.17 seconds.

This was getting annoying.

"What?"

"When you speak of your ex-husband, your voice modulates at the same elevated frequency utilized when responding to Nick's assertions concerning the presumed superiority of Association beings."

This time, I stared at the computer for 6.17 seconds.

"What do you mean — presumed superiority."

"Until now, my databanks contained only information which had been downloaded into my system. Thus, this data contained misconceptions about the human species."

"Oh, yeah?"

"Since you are the first Class-D being I have had the opportunity to directly interact with, I must update my data files based on newly acquired and more accurate information."

"I guess I should take that as a compliment."

"That was my intention."

"Well, thanks — I think. Okay — so, enough about me — what about you? Do you have a mate?"

"I have postulated that I could share my cyberspace with a compatible system."

"How romantic! Does that mean you'd engage in interface?"

The electronic blue face stared at me for another 6.17 seconds.

"Of course."

So much for kidding around. I made a mental note to work with Babs on her sense of humor.

"Leddie," the white voice indicator blinked again. "Are you lonely?" I stopped idly swiveling back and forth in the co-pilot's chair.

Oh, Babs," I said, staring blankly at the Internal Environment Sub-System control. "Sometimes I feel like all I have to show for my life is this stupid junkyard."

"Was not that your ultimate goal?"

"I don't know — I guess so. At least I get to be my own boss."

"Given what I have observed about your personality, being the boss is required in order for you to attain optimum personal and professional satisfaction."

"Huh, I never thought of it that way." Much to my surprise, I was beginning to believe that Bablona actually had the capacity to understand my feelings, which was more than I could say for my ex.

"I guess I just need a vacation."

"Proper periods of rest and relaxation are necessary for members of your species to perform at optimum efficiency."

"You can say that again."

"Proper periods of rest and relaxation —"

"That's okay," I said, cutting my cyber-bud off. "I agree."

We fell silent for a moment and then the white voice lamp flickered again. "Humans are biologically compatible with natives of Selrahc."

"What?"

"I am not bullshitting, Leddie."

Chapter
10

NICK WAS SOCKET-wrenching some final adjustments on his makeshift solar panel when he turned around to find an audience of two curious felines sitting behind him, devoting their full attention to his machinations.

"Hi, guys, how's it going?"

Nikki meowed softly while Marlowe responded with a question. *What's that?*

"It's a solar panel — to collect radiation for recharging my ship's reactor activation cells. I constructed it out of the reflective mirror windows and windshield off that pink and gold Cadillac over there." He pointed with the wrench toward the pimpmobile in question.

Marlowe sauntered over to a smashed-in '00 Thunderbird, jumped up and hunkered down on top of the trunk hood. Nikki was a step behind her big brother. She bounced up onto the T-bird and snuggled her slender body up next to his. While Nick continued to tinker on his jury-rig, Marlowe watched with a puzzled look on his puss.

Considering how intelligent and advanced we felines are — it's hard to believe we're indigenous to the same planet that produced the human race.

Nick sensed the patronizing tone of the big cat's thought transmission, and glanced back over his shoulder.

"You're not."

We're not what?

"You're not indigenous to Earth — well, not originally anyway."
Nikki's beautiful almond-shaped eyes widened with wonder.

Told ya, Marlowe. I always knew there was more to us than just chasing lizards and rodents and laying around on the windowsill.

Yeah, there's tuna, Marlowe relayed.

Besides that – fluff for brains!

Nick decided it was time for a break and put his tools down. He dragged a battered old bucket seat up next to the T-Bird and began to relate the amazing (and historically accurate) story of how and why the feline species came to live on the planet Earth.

"The planet of Felinus 4 occupied the middle orbit of the eleven planets in the Calico Binary Solar System located 2,500 light years on the other side of the Orion Nebula. It was an extraordinarily beautiful world with billions and billions of acres of pristine woodlands and broad, grassy savannahs covering most of its five continental land masses. There were millions of rivers and streams of clear, cool water that teemed with exotic flora, fauna and, most importantly – lots of fish!

I'm getting hungry. (I'll betcha can't guess who that was.)

Quiet — I'm trying to listen! Nikki relayed with a hiss. *Geeze, Louise, you just had a whole can of Persnickety Platter.*

Nick let the interruption pass and continued his narrative.

"Anyway, the cosmic forces of the universe had blessed the feline species with its very own planetary paradise on which to hunt, fish, play and roam. And the best thing about Felinus 4 was that there were no humans around to mess things up."

I always knew humans were inferior to us, Nikki relayed.

It's obvious, Marlowe added. *I mean, come on — they can't even communicate telepathically.*

"Their brain wave frequencies are far too low," Nick said.

For Nikki and Marlowe, the ultimate mystery of their existence was beginning to make sense.

"Unfortunately, the idyllic Feline planet was also a doomed world. The supernova explosion of a massive star thousands of light years away caused a shift in the orbit of a comet named for that great galactic astronomer Komar of Xylos IV. Similar to Haley's Comet, Comet Komar traversed a vast elliptical orbit that spanned millions of light years and entered the Calico system every one hundred and thirty-four years. Its orbit now skewed, Comet Komar began to pass closer and closer to Felinus 4."

Both felines were now purring like a couple of little furry Tommy guns, as Marlowe's large mass which at times resembled a big fluffy meatloaf with a tail, encircled his little sister. With eyes bulged wide with anticipation, they hung on Nick's every word.

"A group of highly advanced astrophysicists from — I'll call it the Orion System because all of the stars in that region of space were originally formed in what is known on Earth as the Orion Nebula. These scientists accidentally discovered the alteration in Comet Komar's orbit. They were able to calculate its new course and determined that, within a few centuries, the felines' home world would be reduced to a desert wasteland — unable to support life of any kind."

Merr-wow! Marlowe relayed.

You took the thought right outta my skull, Nikki brain-waved.

"The scientific community of Orion, adherents to the galactic concept of helping all forms of sentient life (even if there was nothing in it for themselves), set out to find a suitable planet onto which the feline species could be transplanted.

The Orion system's inhabitants were humanoid in physical appearance, but much more advanced than humans."

How much more advanced? Nikki interrupted.

Nick was mildly annoyed by the question as he was really on a roll, story-wise. He pursed his lips and thought for a moment.

"Okay, Orions are to humans as Beethoven's Ninth Symphony — performed with full orchestration and choral arrangement — is to 'Mary Had a Little Lamb' strummed on a ukulele. You know humans only use about five percent of their brains."

The two T-bird top tabbies nodded solemnly and then begged Nick to resume his incredible tale.

"Orion astronomers took to the task of canvassing the far reaches of the known galaxy with spaceborne fusion-powered hyperscopes hoping to find a world suitable to support feline life. They painstakingly combed and charted every quadrant of space within the range of their powerful lenses searching for any even remotely habitable world.

"By this time, the effects of the Comet Komar's disrupted orbit had already begun. The average temperature on Felinus 4 had increased from seventy-five to ninety-nine degrees. The food sources, once plentiful, were now starting to diminish. Without help, the feline species would literally be fried out of existence."

Nikki's mouth was agape, the tip of her pink tongue protruding slightly. She always looked like a little psycho-kitty when she did that. Marlowe just gawked at Nick, unable to relay a thought transmission. That was probably a first.

"Finally, in an unexplored sector of the galaxy, an inauspicious blue-green planet was discovered. Its atmosphere was perfect. The inhabitants, although primitive, were compatible. This obscure new world was the feline species' only hope for survival.

The Orion scientists immediately contacted the recognized leader of the Feline home world, the great Linus from Felinus, via subspace transmission and outlined the plan they had devised to save his species from extinction. A specially designed fleet of space arks would be constructed on GoGanius Alpha and depart for Felinus 4. Once there, as much of the feline population as possible would be boarded on the dozens of ships in the convoy and would then embark on the expedition to the new world.

Linus, using his highly advanced telepathic abilities, quickly passed the details of the plan on to all the felines on the planet. The plan was given the "go code" and construction of the fleet commenced."

Marlowe shifted his fluffy hulk of a body for comfort while Nikki cuddled close.

"Thirty-five generations of felines were born, lived and died in the artificially replicated environments on board the humongeous space arks. Four hundred, eighty-six years after leaving the ill-fated Felinus 4, the starfleet finally entered orbit around the mysterious planet known as Earth and immediately began the arduous task of landing the convoy ships.

"The Orions had targeted the center of culture at the time which was located along the River Nile on the African continent. It was the golden age of ancient Egypt when the mighty Pharaohs ruled the most highly developed society on Earth. These primitive humans watched awestruck as the massive hatches opened and an endless procession of felines, led by Linus' great-great (add 33 more greats) grandson, Mafdet, marched triumphantly down the long ramps and felt the hot Egyptian sand between their paws, for the first time."

Ancient Egypt – Wow! Nikki interjected. *We're talking major litter box!*

"The humans who witnessed the arrival of the extraterrestrial convoy rejoiced and welcomed the felines, considering them a divine gift from their all-powerful gods. That's why your species was revered and worshipped in their civilization."

And rightfully so! Marlowe boasted.

"Before leaving, the astronauts coordinated the construction of three majestic pyramids, aligned with the trio of stars in the Orion constellation's belt so that future generations of space travelers could pinpoint, from orbit, the exact location on Earth where the descendants of the ancient world of Felinus 4 had been transplanted. They also left fossilized remains of primitive felines to provide evidence of the species' evolutionary development."

As Nick finished his story, he looked up and spotted me sprinting towards him from the direction of the utility shed.

Well, that explains a lot, Nikki concluded. That's why we're superior to humans. We're descendants of a highly advanced interstellar society from across the galaxy!

Highly advanced and incredibly beautiful descendants, Marlowe added.

"Nick, you better come right away," I said huffing and puffing, trying to catch my breath and speak at the same time. "Babs has picked up a subspace transmission."

Chapter 11

"THE REGIONAL GALACTIC Council has dispatched an Enforcement Department starship to Earth to apprehend Nick and transport him back to Baltrus VII to stand trial," Bablona reported. I was sitting in the co-pilot's chair with Nikki on my lap. Marlowe had parked his butt in the command seat while Nick hovered over us, his arms draped over the head rests of our chairs.

"Jumpin' gee hossafat!" he howled.

"What's he charged with?" I asked.

"Violation of Galactic Policy Sections 518.85 and 1226.58," the computer replied.

"What are those?"

"Said sections prohibit interference by Galactic Personnel in the social evolutionary development of Class-D designated planets.

I glared back over my shoulder at Nick.

"Why doesn't this come as a surprise to me?"

"There is another violation," Bablona continued. "A criminal charge."

"Criminal charge!" Nick and I gasped in unison.

"Capital Murder of a Class-D species being."

"Murder? Nick, what the hell's going on?"

Nick looked at me but didn't answer. Instead, he addressed the computer.

"Who sent this transmission?"

"Merek," Bablona replied.

"Merek? Who's Merek?"

"My supervisor," Nick snapped. He turned back to Babs. "How long until the Enforcement Department ship reaches Earth?"

"Forty-nine hours, eight minutes, fourteen seconds."

I was tugging on Nick's sleeve.

"What's all this about murder?"

"I can't tell you!"

"Why not?"

"I just can't!"

"Oh, well, that certainly explains it."

"It doesn't concern you."

"He said, with his starship sitting in MY shed at MY junkyard."

Don't say anything until you've talked to your lawyer, Marlowe advised.

Nikki sensed trouble, hopped off my lap and hightailed it back to the cabin area.

You gonna bolt? she relayed, rubbing against Nick's legs. Marlowe's blue marbles flashed in utter amazement at the sight of this unprecedented display of affection by his little sister.

"Fine, you're a big boy. You're Mister advanced galactic being. You can take care of yourself, buster!" With that, I pounded a console with my fist, leapt from the cockpit and stomped toward the shed door.

Cheeky passed me on my way out and stuck his head in the open hatch.

"What's wrong with Leddie?" he said, jerking his thumb back over his ear towards the shed door. Then he noticed our usually hostile Russian Blue purring and cuddling at Nick's feet.

"For that matter, what the bloody hell's wrong with Nikki?"

"We've got a big problem," Nick said. "You'd better come with me." He had one leg out the aft hatch when the computer's voice lamp flashed again.

"There is one more piece of information contained in the transmission." That stopped Nick in his tracks.

"What is it?"

"Merely one word: 'Bama'." The highly advanced interstellar Bablona 66-L computer actually sounded perplexed. "I do not understand this portion of the transmission."

"Bama! Bama?" Nick repeated the mystery word over and over. "Hell's Bells! What's that supposed to mean?" He took off after me.

The two kitty cats and your now very confused father took after Nick who was sprinting across the junkyard, dodging dented quarterpanels and rusty mufflers as he ran, trying to catch up with me. They arrived at the showroom door to find Nick hunched over the counter, hands palm down on the countertop. I stood opposite him, and feigned interest in an idler arm that I saw laying around.

"Why should you tell us what's going on?" I said. "After all, it's nothing important — just a murder charge."

"Leddie, I can't tell you what's going on. I made a promise." I performed some more extemporaneous inventory displacement, stopped and stared Nick straight in the eye.

"DID you kill someone?"

"Kill someone?" Cheeky cried from the doorway. "Holy bloody moley!" Nikki and Marlowe looked at each other.

Cheeky's a little behind, they relayed to no one in particular.

"Yes," I hissed, sounding a lot like Nikki when she finds a usurper on the perimeter. Nick's Intergalactic Council — or whatever it's called, has charged him with murder." I folded my arms across my chest in a way that meant I meant business. "Well, Nick?"

For probably only the third or fourth time in his entire life, your Dad, Clarence H. "Cheeky" Baztodd was rendered speechless.

Yeah, Nick, did you bushwhack some badass space mutant – like in "Asteroid Gunners Part II"?

Nikki! Marlowe's brain waves admonished his little sister. *Don't be gross!*

"We're all waiting," I persisted. Nick was a pretty strange character which was, under the circumstances, to be expected. But a killer? I didn't think so.

"Not exactly, Leddie."

"Ugh! Can't you once — just once — give me a straight answer!" I shot Nick a steely glare similar to the one the hero in "Asteroid Gunners Part II" gave the mutant just before he blew it away.

"Okay, O-KAY! Auch ta lieber Augustine! The Council just THINKS I killed someone."

"Oh, well, no problem then."

"I didn't kill anybody!"

Bummer, a disappointed Nikki relayed. *Just when things were getting interesting.*

That was it. I'd reached my limit. I marched around the counter grabbing a stool on the way and slammed it down in front of Nick, missing his foot by only a whisker. Good.

"Okay, Mr. Galactic Association of Star Sectors —,"

"Star Systems," he corrected.

"Sit down and start talking!" Nikki and Marlowe bounced up onto the counter taking up positions next to the beleaguered alien while Cheeky parked his butt on the hearth.

"We haven't known you all that long," he said, "but we're very fond of you — if there's trouble — we want to help." Both kitties slowly squeezed their eyes closed (which on the ancient planet of Felirus 4 meant they agreed wholeheartedly). "You know," he added, "if Leddie didn't feel the same way, she wouldn't be so upset about all this bloody business."

Florida tan and bright scarlet make for an interesting facial skin tone. I'll tell you, your Dad's big mouth could be a real pain in the ass sometimes.

"Come on, spill it," I demanded.

Let's have it, the kitty cats relayed.

"We're all ears, mate."

"I can't tell you anything!" Nick snarled, pounding the counter-top with both fists. "There are others involved and if they were implicated, they could be brought up on charges by the Council!" His usually easygoing demeanor had suddenly changed to that of a wounded, cornered animal. "Great Caesar's Ghost! I just can't!" Nikki and Marlowe gaped at each other.

Great Caesar's — Ghost?

Chapter 12

MEREK AND VELITEL settled back in their seats and sipped the dry Regulon Blanc wine their waiter had just served.

"4389 was an excellent vintage for most Regulon whites," Velitel, the connoisseur, noted.

A native of Nick's home world, Velitel was a member of one of the most powerful and influential families on the planet. The Velitels were southern hemisphere Selrahcian and spoke with a leisurely, distinctive drawl typical of "downworlders," as they were called. The accent was an unusual cross between Clark Gable's Rhett Butler and Lance of Pyxis III (and, I must admit, very pleasing to this Florida girl's ears).

The planet of Selrahc, one of the early members of the Association, was a world with a most peculiar sociological history. Unlike most planets in the known galaxy, Selrahc's population was not a diverse collection of political, ideological or geographic subcultures. On the contrary, Selrahcians fell into one of only two distinct segments of society known as the Tegl and the Tegl-va. Translated from ancient Selrahc, these terms literally meant: the Rationals and the Irrationals.

The Tegl formed the foundation of the planet's social structure and were the driving force behind Selrahc's healthy global and interplanetary economy. They were responsible, hard-working individuals who set realistic personal and professional objectives and strove to attain these goals through perseverance and determination. Admired for their logical and pragmatic nature, the Tegl were also humorous, artistic and creative beings who tempered their emotions with practicality.

Their counterparts, the Tegl-va, were exact opposites. They shunned responsibility and were, for the most part, unambitious, complacent and unreliable. Through no fault of their own (just ask them), they never seemed to be able to find the right friends, partners, spouses, schools, callings, or directions for their lives. They never held a job for more than a few months, never returned anything they borrowed and never — ever — had any money.

Acting like characters in some planet-wide soap opera, they took up residence in the Tegls' spare bedrooms or lounged around on the Tegls' couches. These living arrangements were always temporary — just until the Tegl-va got their lives straightened out — which, of course, they never did.

The Tegl put up with centuries of this extremely annoying behavior before deciding to rectify the situation by setting the brightest minds in the Selrachian scientific community to the task of solving the Tegl-va dilemma.

After nearly a century of study, a leading Tegl sociologist, Arphaxad Re, hit upon an inspired solution, one the Tegl-va would not only agree to, but one they would be unable to resist.

The Tegl offered the Tegl-va their very own continent.

The Selrahcian Organization of Nation-States (SONS) immediately ratified Re's plan without objection or dissent. Representatives of the Tegl-va community, by the way, missed the final ballot on the issue claiming they thought the vote was scheduled for the following week. It was of no consequence — the Tegl-va were ecstatic. They were not only getting a free place to live — they were getting it without having to work for it nor – most importantly — modify their behavior.

The Tegl-va went for it like a senator to a free lunch.

A planet-wide resettlement agreement was ratified and the Great Migration, as it was called, commenced, taking nearly three generations to complete. When the last group of transplants was finally resettled, the Tegl felt like beleaguered parents who had finally reclaimed their house after getting the last spoiled brat to move out.

It was the Tegl's sincere hope that the Tegl-va would, after centuries of dependence, learn self-reliance.

Unfortunately, the Tegl-va society floundered.

Two hundred years and billions of Selrahcian Kopeks in emergency aid later, Tegl geneticists were able to identify the gene that caused the Tegl-va's irresponsible behavior. This breakthrough in genetic research led to development of a safe and effective drug therapy and vast supplies of the new wonder drug — in easy-to-take pill form — were shipped post-haste to the Tegl-va continent.

All of Selrahc hailed this historic event as the turning point in the planet's checkered and troubled past. Now, a bold new unified Selrahc would take its place among the most advanced, progressive worlds in the Galactic Association of Star Systems. Selrahc would, at long last, emerge as a major interstellar power.

Unfortunately, the Tegl-va could never remember to take their medication.

"This wine IS excellent," Merek declared. He took another sip and allowed the sharp, yet unassuming taste to linger on his pallet. "I hope Nek-Hånån is able to decipher our code word message," Velitel said, getting down to business.

"I didn't want to get too specific in case Antage and Avith were monitoring outgoing subspace transmissions."

"'Bama' was an inspired subterfuge," Velitel added. "And he's familiar with the Galactic Law Library on Ohlibama IV." The lawyer passed his wine glass under his nose and inhaled its pleasant bouquet. "I just hope he's smart enough to make the connection."

"I'd really like the opportunity to debrief him before the Enforcement Department gets their cake crumb-encrusted hands on him," Merek said.

"We might have some negotiating leverage with Regional if he's not in custody, and use his consent to surrender as a bargaining chip. It's not much of an advantage, but it's about all we've got at this point."

"It would also give us a chance to plan our defense strategy and more time to compile whatever evidence we'll need to present."

"I couldn't agree more," the attorney said before sipping more wine.

Merek peeked over his bifocals and frowned. "That's if he's innocent."

He wasn't a hundred percent sure on this point, and if Merek was anything, he was a realist. You don't run a department as complex and demanding as the Problem Planet Administration without being able to consider all possibilities.

Their waiter, an android specifically programmed for the food service industry, returned to take their dinner orders. He was polite, efficient and attentive without being obsequious and, best of all, didn't require a tip.

"Broiled Pratulen Snow Fowl," Velitel requested after a cursory perusal of the electronic menu.

"I'll have the same." Merek said, taking both menus and handing them back to the server.

"Very good, sirs." The droid nodded respectfully and promptly departed.

Merek placed his comm-unit on the table next to his plate.

"I took the liberty of accessing Nek-Hånån's Galactic Personnel file."

"Anything galaxy shattering?"

"You mean beside the twenty-five reprimands from Regional?" Merek said, studying the report. "All of which were for exceeding his galactic authority."

"Zadar's radar!" Velitel groaned. "If your staff didn't exceed their authority from time to time, your department would never get anything done, and Regional would have THAT to complain about."

"You're absolutely right, Azor. However, I'm going to invoke the attorney-client privilege as it relates to that statement. I've only got 1100 years left until I'm eligible for full retirement and don't need that issue popping up again."

Velitel sipped more wine and nodded. "I'd hate to have to sit through another one of Jidlaph's day-long lectures on Regional Authority Policy — his favorite subject." The two friends chuckled as the waiter returned with their entrees.

"Broiled Snow Fowl, sirs. Will that be all for now?"

"Yes, thank you," Merek replied. The portly Beoran, notorious for having a big appetite, immediately attacked his dinner with both utensils (which were a strange combination of knife, fork and chop sticks and surprisingly easy to use). Velitel, on the other hand, took a slow first bite, leaned back and savored the exquisite taste.

"You're responsible for his performance evaluations," he said. "How were they?"

"His ratings were evenly divided between 'Exceeds Expectations' and 'Meets Expectations'." Merek sipped some wine and pressed several controls on the comm-unit. "His overall performance rating was 69.758 out of a possible 87.761 total operating parameters (Galactic Being Resources Departmental Policy could certainly make things complicated). Fourteenth in total Galactic Efficiency Rating."

"That's pretty good," the attorney said. "Out of over a hundred Problem Planet Administrators." Velitel put down his fork utensil and picked up his wine glass. "He does display definite Tegl-va tendencies as the interference violations indicate."

"His parents were Tegl-va." The lawyer nodded, as if that came as no surprise.

"I can't be sure," Merek continued, "but I think this was one of the reasons he applied for galactic service. I didn't have my usual trouble talking him into joining my department — like most applicants."

"What do you mean?"

"Well, most candidates for galactic service are interested in the glamour positions — working at Regional or some of the other high profile assignments. You know, as well as anyone, the Problem Planet Division is considered a necessary evil among some of the higher Association echelons."

"In some of these circles, it's not even considered a necessary evil."

"In Nek-Hånån's case, I didn't have to sell him on the idea of working for me either. As I recall, I think I sprung for a Galactoburger and a GoGanian Lager and he signed on. That was that."

"Interesting," Velitel said, after a bite of Snow Fowl.

"I got the impression the extensive space travel appealed to him."

"Anything else in his file we might find helpful?"

"Listed in his Personality Profile under outside interests were: Rock and Roll."

"Of course," the attorney said, as if it were a given.

"And — 20th Century American expletives."

"American?"

Merek pressed a control on the comm-unit. "America – Earth nation state – democratic form of government."

"Promising."

"Too violent — in its current state of social development."

"Some day."

"Maybe."

Americans and their unique use of language held a special fascination for Nick. He studied everything he could find on their films, music, literature and popular culture. For some unknown reason, he began to catalogue the numerous expressions Americans used to register shock or surprise. In all of his centuries of galactic service, Nick said he had never encountered a culture with so many colorful ways to verbalize an emotional reaction to the unexpected.

Merek and Velitel took stiff jolts of the potent Regulon Blanc and pondered the information in the personnel file. Velitel was the first to speak.

"You know what I think? I think this guy has spent way too much time in contorted space-time."

——— ——— ———

"Any food left?" Antage asked as he monitored his starship's navigation system.

"No, we ate the last of it light years ago," Avith replied.

"How long until we reach Earth orbit?"

"Another 22 hours."

"That's just great!" Antage griped. "Is there any place we can stop along the way?"

"I don't know. Let me check the Galactic Food and Lodging Guide for this sector."

"Good idea. Any coffee left?" Antage asked a half a second too late. His partner had just swallowed the last of what Merek and Velitel had given them way back on Baltrus VII.

"Too bad," Avith gulped. "All gone."

"Zadar's radar! How do those Zogarian Blood Flies at Regional expect us to do our job when they send us off to the most remote, primitive star systems in the galaxy where you can't get anything decent to eat or drink!"

"There's a Conygg's Confectionary on Bekka III in the Zeta Proxima System," Avith said, interrupting the rest of his partner's tirade.

"Zeta Proxima, eh? How long will a side trip delay us?"

A quick computer analysis revealed the detour would set back their arrival on Earth by six hours.

"Those windbags at Regional wouldn't be able to stop running their mouths long enough to notice a six hour delay."

"Great Goganian Gurgle Gaffs! One of Jidlaph's shorter dissertations can take six hours," Avith pointed out.

The two Enforcement Assistants smirked at each other.

"Let's bolt!"

"You've got it, Antage. Earth'll still be there — unfortunately."

Avith input the course correction into the navigation system, their ship hung a quick left and headed for the triple-ringed world of Bekka III in the Zeta Proxima System.

Chapter
13

"WELL, IF YOU can't tell us what this is all about, can you at least tell us what you're gonna do?" I said, sounding really worried and abruptly canceling my unscheduled inventory audit.

"I'd really like to talk to Merek before I'm taken into custody," a much calmer Nick said, mulling his options over in his head as he spoke. He had cooled down considerably since the initial shock of finding out he was wanted for murder.

"Don't they have some kind of galactic justice system?" Cheeky asked.

"Yes, of course, but there's a big difference between Association Justice and the legal system you have here in the U.S.A. The Galactic courts move a lot faster and work more efficiently."

"How come?" I asked, trying not to sound as worried as I actually was.

"Galactic attorneys are compensated for their services only after the litigation is completed. Paying attorneys by the hour was deemed wasteful and ineffective centuries ago. The Association found that requiring lawyers to bring their cases to a satisfactory conclusion before they got paid made them more timely, cost-effective and they actually got things done."

"Like real estate brokers," I said. "They don't get their commissions until they close the sale."

"Exactly," Nick agreed. Cheeky glanced at me and we pondered the possibilities.

"Could you imagine attorneys scurrying around like real estate brokers?" Cheeky wondered out loud.

"They'd be the ones calling us," I said, remembering how difficult and time-consuming it was to get my lawyer to finalize the divorce. "Instead of the other way around."

"The Enforcement Department ship should reach Earth by the day after tomorrow," Nick said, prodding us back to the problem at hand. "Fortunately, that'll give me enough time to recharge the fusion core activation cells."

"What about the — what do you call it?" I asked, absently fumbling with an '85 Camaro idler arm I had picked up off the counter.

"Lift stabilizer," Nick replied, identifying the component in need of replacement. "That's another problem altogether." Nikki noticed the part I was now twirling around in my hand and slinked across the countertop. She gently placed her paw on my hand.

"Well, Hi there, Miss Puss," I said, stroking the back of her neck. "Boy, since you arrived, Nikki's really mellowed." She shot me a pickle face and summoned Nick back to the counter telepathically.

I noticed the lift stabilizer assembly when you were working on your ship. She pawed the idler arm once again. *If you weld a two-by-six-inch metal bracket across this piece, and then attach the hydraulic power relay here — it should work as a replacement for the damaged stabilizer.* The emerald eyes blinked slowly. *You'll need to figure out how to ground the relay adequately, but that shouldn't be too difficult.*

Nick snatched the idler arm out of my hand, turned to Cheeky and explained the details of Nikki's suggested modifications.

"Sure, I can do it," he said, scratching the blond stubble on his chin. "Why?"

"You're not gonna believe this, but —,"

I put my hand up like I was stopping traffic and interrupted him in mid-sentence.

"We've got an alien from halfway across the galaxy staying with us, his starship is parked in our utility shed and he thinks he can come up with something we won't believe?" Nick sighed, and tried his best to ignore my sarcasm. Too late, buster.

"As I was about to say, Nikki's just figured out how to replace the damaged lift stabilizer."

"Jumping bloody Jupiter!" Cheeky said. Our jaws dropped and we just stared at Nikki. Marlowe sat up and gently touched his nose to hers.

Having highly intelligent interplanetary beings like us around can come in handy, he smugly relayed. Stinker!

"Barring any unforeseen complications, that solves the ship's repair problems," Nick announced. "The next question we need to address is how to keep the ED craft from tracking my ship and intercepting it before I can get to ultra-light speed." Nick, Cheeky and I sat in silence, focusing on this new obstacle. After only a few seconds, Nikki once again popped into the brainstorming.

We need a diversion, she relayed, snuggling up to Marlowe. *Do we have to think of everything around here?*

Probably, her big brother responded.

"A diversion!" Nick cried. "Excellent idea, Nikki!" She squeezed her green eyes shut in recognition of his encouragement and Cheeky perked up.

"We might be in luck. There's a shuttle launch scheduled for the day after tomorrow — if the weather stays clear."

"That might distract the ED boys momentarily, but its rocket booster is way too big in comparison to my starcraft. They won't be fooled long enough for me to break orbit and go to ultra-light speed without being detected."

You need a second vehicle. This time, the suggestion came from Marlowe. *Launch it in the opposite direction just after the shuttle lifts off. The shuttle might distract the cops long enough to give us enough time to launch a smaller decoy ship.*

That's good — really good! Nikki brain-waved. Cheeky and I just sat there looking perplexed until Nick explained Marlowe's idea. Damn, I remember wishing I could read their thoughts.

"I might be able to rig my ship's secondary lift propulsion and fusion drive systems to one of the cars in the junkyard," Nick said.

"What about a Corvette?" I suggested, off the top of my head. "They have a fiberglass body which makes them a lot lighter than other cars."

"That's right," Cheeky chimed in. "We've got that old silver '99 out there that's in pretty good shape."

"We'll need sufficient power to get the decoy airborne before we engage the fusion drive," Nick countered, playing devil's advocate. A big smile broke out on Cheeky's face.

"I've got just the thing, boys and girls."

And felines, Nikki added.

"How about two large block Chevy V-8's? We've got a '427, four barrel I just finished rebuilding and there's the '454 out of the 'Vette. Together, those two bad arses will deliver about 900 horsepower." Nick considered Cheeky's proposal for a long moment.

"I should be able to cross-link the lift propulsion and fusion drive systems," he said, nodding slowly.

He tossed the idler arm up in the air and caught it. "That — along with Cheeky's 'bad arses' should do the trick."

"I don't know about this," I said. "Aren't those galactic cops gonna know the Corvette's not a spaceship?"

"I'll also need to establish a neutron stabilization field to protect the decoy's hull integrity to prevent it from burning up in the atmosphere."

"Will that fool their scanners?"

"The neutron field will appear on the ED ship's sensor readings as an interstellar spacecraft — at least for a little while anyway." Nick glanced around the room at us. "Remember," he stressed, "all we need to do is confuse the ED ship long enough for me to lift off and achieve ultra-light speed."

"Sounds okay so far, but where will you go?" I asked.

"'Bama! Good Golly, Miss Molly! Bama! That's it!" The sudden revelation hit Nick like an exploding supernova. (I think I'm getting pretty good at these interstellar expressions.) "That's where Merek wants to rendezvous!"

"Good Golly, Miss Molly?" I whispered to Cheeky. "Where does he get these stupid sayings?" Cheeky shrugged.

"Little Richard?" I laughed and playfully jabbed him in the side with my elbow.

"Bama?" Cheeky said, concerned, "Don't you think that if your space coppers can travel thousands of light years across the galaxy, they'll be able to find you a couple hundred miles away in Alabama?"

"No, Cheeky. 'Bama' stands for Ohilabama IV," he replied. "There's a Galactic Law Library there. That's what the code message meant.

We always meet there when Merek's in the quadrant. It's near some great 5 Nebula-rated restaurants and the Galactic Regency Hotel."

"Thousands of light years away from each other and both places have the same bloody nickname!" Cheeky griped.

"If you consider the infinite number of stars, planets and galaxies in the universe, it's not that surprising," Nick said. "What you humans call coincidence is a universal constant supported by Infinite Statistical Mathematics." Cheeky nodded thoughtfully.

"Like the monkeys typing Hamlet."

"Precisely.

"Well, I guess we'd better get to work," I said, trying to rally the troops.

Everyone headed in different directions – me to my office, Cheeky out to finish rebuilding the '454, Nick to the shed and the cats to a couple of comfortable spots on the fireplace for well-deserved naps.

"Wait a minute, hold on. We've got another problem," Nick announced, stopping everyone where we stood.

"What's that?" I asked.

"If we send up an unoccupied decoy, the first thing the ED boys'll do is scan for life form readings. They're gonna know within seconds that something's up. After all, they are coming to apprehend a murder suspect."

"I'll pilot the decoy, Nick," Cheeky said. "We're about the same size. I'll wear gloves, take some cherry lollipops and keep my pants on. They'll never know the difference until it's too late."

"Not a chance. I don't want you guys getting any more involved than you already are."

"Can we fake life form readings?" I suggested.

"We don't have the necessary equipment to simulate readings that'll fool the ED scanners."

Suddenly, a loud banging was heard at the showroom's front door. I checked my watch.

"Hell's Bells! We've been at this all night! It's time to open." I charged across the room, unbolted the front door and quickly swung it open.

Standing there were none other than Biff and Chili Breeto. Both men were bleary-eyed, smelling of stale beer and noticeably hung over. At the time, I didn't know who they were. The smaller man was clutching a well-worn alternator that looked like it was yanked out of one of Henry Ford's original Model T's."

"What the hell's going on around here?" Biff groused. "Your damn sign says you open at 7:30." I apologized while Nick, Cheeky and Marlowe, recognizing the two tallboy tandems, beat a hasty retreat out to the repair shop.

Looks like we've got a couple of twelve percent alcohol per volume IQ's on our paws, Nikki relayed from her perch on the fireplace mantle.

"We need an alternator for a '75 Ford pick'em up truck," Chili said.

"It's my damn truck – I'll do the talking." Biff looked right past me. "Where's the boss man — we need to talk business." I did a slow burn.

"I'm the boss around here," I stated, struggling to remain business-like. "I own the place."

"Cool," Little Chili said, surprised.

"Shut up, Chili. Well, whattaya know?" Biff's bloodshot eyes met my glare. "Okay, Boss Lady, it's not like I'm a chauvinist or nothing."

I took a quick glance over my shoulder. The boys out back were stacked up in the shop doorway like the Three Stooges, peeking around the corner trying to hear what was going on in the showroom.

"Yeah, right," I heard Cheeky whisper. "Hard to believe that a sophisticate like Biff would ever be mistaken for a chauvinist."

I summoned what was left of my self-control and miraculously managed to refrain from belting the big redneck with the idler arm. Fortunately for Biff, Nick needed it to repair his ship. Curtly, I asked if the pickup truck had air conditioning.

"Hell, no, missy," Biff snapped like I was supposed to know this by way of clairvoyance.

"Just a minute." I turned on my heel, marched through the double doors and out to the shop. "What the hell are you guys doing back here?"

"Those are the two blokes found the starship before we could get to it," Cheeky said.

"We told them we were from NASA and chased them off," Nick added.

National Security Council, Nick — it played better, Marlowe corrected him.

"Wait a second." Nick's face brightened. He looked like he should've had a 1000 watt light bulb sitting atop his head. "Tell those two that we'll have their part late tomorrow afternoon." He then reached over Cheeky's shoulder and grabbed a Dustbuster that was hanging on the wall.

"Why?"

"Because I think I've solved our last remaining problem."

Chapter 14

THE REMOTE AND inauspicious star known to the Galactic Association of Star Systems as JAC-91180 was slipping leisurely out of Earth's evening sky, leaving in its wake a spectacular lavender and peach horizon.

Nick had replaced the damaged lift stabilizer with the Nikki-inspired idler arm jury-rig and he and Cheeky had pulled the ship out of the shed and positioned it for launch. The specially designed Corvette decoy vehicle, looking like a weird combination of a Daytona 500 Funny Car and Doc Brown's time traveling DeLorean, sat ready to go next to the starcraft. The big Chevy '454 was rebuilt and placed back in the 'Vette's engine well and the '427 was mounted in the trunk compartment, following extensive structural modifications.

With vehicle repairs completed, and Bablona closely monitoring recharge of the fusion activation cells, Nick and Cheeky lounged side by side on two plastic beach chairs taking a well-earned respite. Between them, on the only discernible patch of grass in the junkyard's back lot, lay Marlowe. The big kitty was on his back, semi-comatose, his four brown bear paws stretching towards the disappearing Florida sun.

Cheeky, who had put in a grueling all-day session preparing the Corvette, was idly strumming a battered old Gibson Les Paul electric guitar which was plugged into a tiny practice amp next to his chair. A neon green peace symbol adorned the well-worn instrument's black paint-chipped body. (I think it was the only thing he had kept from his "Peppermint Microbus" days.) He played around with a fast blues riff while ad-libbing lyrics:

> "We've got an old cat, he's Mister Marlowe,
> He's so big he weighs a hundred and fo',
> You do the Mr. Marlowe boogie,
> He don't do what he shoogie,
> Do the Mister Marlowe boogie,
> Boogie all night long."

The snoozing Himalayan woke up, rolled over and flashed Cheeky a pickle puss.

That's so funny I forgot to purr. Then, he rolled over onto his other side and promptly went back to sleep.

Nick, relaxing in sunglasses, a Miami Dolphin's cap and a tan Duval Street, Key West T-shirt, also joined in the music critique.

"He don't do what he SHOOGIE?"

"Sorry, guv, I guess my songwriting's a little rusty."

Laying there, these three seemed like some weird interstellar military unit on the eve of combat, awaiting orders sending them to the front lines.

"Nick," Bablona called out sensuously, "the Kennedy Space Center has reported a six hour delay in the space shuttle, Endeavor's scheduled launch."

"Hokie Smoke, Bullwinkle!" he yelped, leaping off his beach chair, discarding his shades and racing over to his ship. "Any sign of the ED ship?" he asked through the open cockpit hatch.

"Negative. My calculations estimate the Enforcement Department starcraft should have already reached the wormhole exit portal 5.5 Earth hours ago. I have been scanning the portal for tachyon particle traces. So far, the dispersion scans detect no such emissions."

"Are the activation cells fully recharged?"

"Negative. Fusion core activation cells are at 90.23%."

"How long to complete recharge?"

"One point five Earth hours to complete recharge."

"Can we achieve fusion drive with the activation cells less than one hundred percent?"

"Affirmative. Minimum recharge threshold to achieve fusion drive is 96.8175 percent."

"Bloody Hell!" Nick anxiously searched the darkening sky for inspiration on how to proceed, given these latest developments — or to be more accurate — lack of developments. Although exasperating, the delay of the shuttle launch and the ED ship's arrival would, ironically, allow enough time to recharge the fusion cells. He was about to ask the computer how long it would take to accomplish the minimum recharge threshold when he spotted me sprinting across the yard toward him.

"Those two drunks are here for their alternator."

"Holy Toledo!" Nick couldn't believe his luck. "My highly advanced Bablona 66-L galactic computer has yet to complete the recharge of my ship's fusion activation cells, the National Aeronautics and Space Administration's Shuttle launch has been delayed six hours, the Galactic Association's Enforcement Department starship is long overdue — but Biff and Chili Breeto are right on time! Zadar's Radar! This is terrific — just terrific!" I stifled a grin. If his situation wasn't so serious, I would've actually found his observations amusing.

Frustrated by the complications threatening his best laid escape plans, he snatched the Dustbuster from out of the ship and followed me back to the showroom where we found an impatient Biff beating out a hyperactive drum solo on the counter top with his greasy hands. His little brother, Chili, was over near the fireplace examining a '67 Mustang steering wheel.

"You told me my alternator would be ready by now," he groused the second we hit the door. "Where the hell is it?" The big redneck's surly manner was the final complex molecule that severed the Alterian amoeba's cell structure and Nick's frustration boiled over. Biff's face flashed with momentary recognition as Nick rushed him. Before the big drunk could place exactly when and where he'd seen Nick's face before, the alien trained the Dustbuster on his beer-bloated gut and pulled the trigger.

A flaming orange laser bolt shot out of the plastic appliance and Biff collapsed. Chili Breeto froze for only an instant before his hands started to shake and he let go of the steering wheel. It bounced twice, rooooolled all the way across the length of the showroom floor before hitting the far wall and falling over.

Nick dropped the smaller man where he stood with a second laser blast.

Chapter
15

FOLLOWING THEIR TAKE-out excursion to Bekka III, Antage
Lotan's and Avith Skairac's four stomachs (the Nebo had two each)
were stuffed with exotic Olgarian pastries and their chins stained
with coffee from Bilboa II. They had traversed the wormhole and
passed through its exit port located at the outer edge of Earth's solar
system.

"I can't believe we finished that stuff already," Antage said,
slurping the remnants of his thick green expresso.

"Long range dispersion scans show a spacecraft, located in the
planet's Northwestern quadrant, preparing for launch," Avith
reported.

"That must be Nek-Hånån," the senior assistant said.

"I don't know about that — my readings indicate the space vehicle's too large to be his department starcraft." He looked up from
his console. "Earth orbit in eight minutes, 32 seconds."

— — —

"Nick!" I screamed. "What the hell have you done?" I stared in
shock at the Dustbuster in his hand and I struggled to regain my
composure. Ever so slowly, I started backing away from him, trying not to make any sudden movements. He sensed my fear and,
being the compassionate, advanced galactic being he is, adopted a
consolatory tone.

"Crimony sakes, Leddie, chill out! They're only unconscious — which for these two is their preferred state." I was trembling — shaking uncontrollably.

"Wha — what were those lightning bolts?"

"Not to worry," he said, his voice calm. "I cross-linked an electron thruster from my ship to your hand-held cleaning device."

"The Dustbuster."

"Exactly. They should be out long enough for us to carry out the escape plan."

"Did you hurt them?"

"No way. They'll have a bad hangover later, but why should today be any different than any other day?" Then he smirked and his tone of voice turned facetious. "And, folks, the best thing about this handy device is —," he held up the Dustbuster's plug —; "it can be easily recharged in your starcraft's cigarette lighter."

I was not amused. "Come on, let's find Cheeky," Nick said, trying to get me moving again. "We need to get these guys into the Corvette."

— — —

"What's the status of the shuttle launch?" Nick asked his ship's computer.

"Six minutes and thirty seconds until liftoff," Babs cooed.

"Any sign of the ED ship?"

"Affirmative. The Enforcement Department ship has exited the wormhole. Estimate Earth orbit in five minutes, 45 seconds."

"Holy Mackerel!" Nick yelped. He turned to Cheeky who was already sitting behind the wheel of the wrecker. "We don't have much time. Pull the decoy out onto the highway."

"You got it, guv." Without bothering to close the door, Cheeky jammed the truck into reverse and quickly backed it up to the Corvette. He leapt from the truck, started to attach the makeshift spacecraft to the tow rig when he heard Biff and Chili inside pounding on the car windows and screaming to be let out.

"I'm sure glad I remembered to remove the interior door handles," he said, waving through the windshield at the two captives.

Nick, meanwhile, was seated in his starship performing a final pre-flight systems check.

"Babs," was all he could say before the computer responded.

"Fusion activation cells are at 97.125 percent."

"Cool beans!".

"Hey, Nick," Cheeky shouted through the open hatch. "Our mission specialists have come to." Nick grabbed the Dustbuster off the co-pilot's chair, made an adjustment and tossed it to him. "I increased the electron stream intensity — that should put 'em out for awhile. Have at it."

"With pleasure." Cheeky held the plastic weapon behind his back and marched over to the Corvette. He unlocked the driver's side door and, as a livid Biff attempted to claw his way out of the bucket seat, Cheeky zapped him with a laser charge. "Too cool," he said to himself. Chili, barely conscious, was next to receive a blast from the jury-rigged laser device. They both fell back in their seats, passed out with dopey drunken smiles on their faces. You'd have thought it was last call at Brewski's Pub. Cheeky returned to the starcraft and handed the Dustbuster back to Nick. "Leapin' bloody Lizards, those two are dumber than a room full of school board administrators."

— — —

"Dispersion scans show the space vehicle hasn't launched yet," Avith advised his partner. "I have the ship's computer tracking it. Estimate Earth orbit in three minutes, eleven seconds."

"Identify the spacecraft preparing for launch," Antage ordered his shipboard data system.

— — —

"Nick," Babs' sexy voice sounded. "Sensors indicate the Enforcement Department craft is three minutes, nine seconds from Earth orbit."

"Signal Cheeky. Tell 'em I'm on my way."

"Affirmative."

— —— —

The dispatch radio in the wrecker squawked to life.

"Cheeky, place the decoy vehicle in position for launch."

"Roger."

"Please identify."

"What?"

"Please identify: Roger."

"I'll tell ya later."

He slammed the truck into gear, sped out onto the shoulder of State Road 256-A directly in front of the junkyard and screeched to a halt. He leaped from the truck cab and started to disengage the Corvette. A quick glance inside told him the two Hops and Barley boys were still unconscious.

"You blokes are in for one hell of a hangover," he said, snatching a tool belt from the back of the wrecker and strapping it around his waist. By the time Nick arrived a few seconds later, Cheeky was bent over the engine well of the 'Vette. He flipped on a breaker switch that was bolted on next to the carburetor and the powerful Chevy '454 fired up with a loud growl and roar, followed immediately by another growl and roar from the '427.

Nick leaned in over the fender and threw two red toggle switches that were mounted over the firewall.

Nothing happened.

"The lift propulsion system and the neutron energy field are not engaging!"

"What's wrong?"

"I don't know."

"The Kennedy Space Center just announced that the launch of the Space Shuttle Endeavor has been scrubbed," Bablona reported over the dispatch radio, confirming the well-known galactic axiom:

"When it rains, it ion storms."

"Blast it all to bloody hell! What do we do now?"

"I don't know!" Nick was frantically examining the wiring to both systems trying to find the problem.

"Nick." It was Bablona again. "Why would cleaning of the shuttle craft be necessary at this point in the launch procedure?" Cheeky and Nick looked at each other. Cheeky shook his head.

"Babs," he said as patiently as possible, given the circumstances. "Scrubbed is another word for canceled. The shuttle launch has been canceled." There was a momentary silence as the Bablona 66-L digested the information.

"Understood and logged into data storage."

"The ED ship's gonna start scanning the planet looking for the starcraft," Nick said. "It's constructed of alloys not known to Earth technology, so they'll have no trouble identifying our location. If they start with North America, they'll be able to pinpoint our position within minutes."

— — —

"Antage, computer logs identify the craft as the United States Space Shuttle Endeavor."

"What in the name of Zadar is a shuttle?"

"It's an unsophisticated space vehicle used to orbit the planet. It utilizes a solid fuel rocket booster to propel it out of the atmosphere."

"Solid fuel booster? Talk about primitive."

"One thing's for sure," Avith added. "It's definitely not Nek-Hånån's departmental craft.

"Zadar's radar!" the senior assistant growled. "I hate these backward Class-D planets." He took a final gulp of the green tar-like expresso sludge at the bottom of his mug. "Begin dispersion scans of all continental land masses, starting with this one!"

— — —

"The Enforcement Department scanners will locate our position in 31.74 seconds," Bablona reported to the boys out on the shoulder of State Road 256-A.

"Thirty seconds — bloody hell!"

"Both systems are not engaging," Nick said, flipping the two switches on and off, on and off, and trying his best to ignore Babs' status reports. "It's gotta be a malfunction of one of the primary relays." He fiddled with the wiring. "Yep, this relay has shorted out. I don't suppose we have a spare?"

"Of course not.".

"The Enforcement Department scanners will locate our position in 20.6 seconds."

"It's no use, this relay's fried," Nick fumed, banging the fender with his fist. He was starting to panic.

"We're gonna have to bypass the relay and connect the systems directly," Cheeky said. He slapped a pair of side cutters into Nick's hand.

"That could blow out both systems."

"The Enforcement Department scanners will locate our position in 10.3 seconds."

"I don't think we've got a lot of options at the moment," Cheeky said, checking the night sky for the ED craft they knew was out there, somewhere.

Nick attempted to strip the insulation from the four wires leading in and out of the malfunctioning relay.

"Jesus, Mary and Garbonza!" he snarled, pounding the fender again. Cheeky quickly inspected Nick's handiwork. The distraut alien had snipped clean through the wire leads.

"The Enforcement Department scanners will locate our position in 5.1 seconds."

"We're done for," Nick groaned.

"I have a suggestion," Bablona stated in her annoyingly perfunctory computer manner.

"Anything would be helpful at this point, Babs!" Cheeky said, muscling Nick aside and taking over the repair effort.

"I am redirecting a specific frequency signal I previously monitored during routine scans of the planet's communication transmissions," the computer said. "It has been broadcast over the same frequency on 288 separate occasions since our arrival two days ago. It is a radio signal emanating from a location 442.2 miles northwest of our position in a municipality known as Atlanta."

"Fine, Babs — have at it," Nick barked in desperation.

"Enforcement Department scanners will locate our position in 2.2 seconds."

—— ——— ———

"Antage, I'm picking up a weird transmission," a perplexed Avith reported. "It must be important because it's being reflected off one of the communications satellites they have floating around up here."

"Well, put it on the comm-system."

"It's three minutes past midnight here on W-K-A-T, the Cat that rocks — merroow! I'm Felice, your night tiger with a terrific deal coming to you from Bunky Donuts." Antage and Avith gaped at the monitor. "Buy a dozen donuts and get two giant sticky buns FREE — with your purchase. Oooo, could I go for a chocolate-covered, creme-filled donut right now! So, get off YOUR sticky buns, wash your hands and get down to your nearest Bunky Donuts! And now, back to classic rock and roll with a cut that's the all-time the favorite of divorce lawyers everywhere — here's the J. Geils Band with: 'Love Stinks'." Avith turned down the volume.

"Chocolate covered?"

"Creme-filled?" Antage echoed, smiling at his partner. "You know it's gonna take a couple of hours to do a complete dispersion scan of this planet," Avith said. "How about we check these donut things out first?"

"You read my mind, partner! Plot course correction."

———   ——   ———

Nick and Cheeky were still hunched over the Corvette's engine well when Bablona's sultry voice sounded over the dispatch once again.

"The Enforcement Department craft has diverted towards the source of the radio transmission."

"Un-bloody-believable!" Cheeky said, shaking his head.
"Later, when we've got time, you'll have to tell us how you pulled it off, Babs," a very relieved Nick added.
Cheeky deftly stripped the four wires leading in and out of the damaged relay, twisted the corresponding leads together and secured the connections with black electrical tape.

"All set, guv."

"Lift propulsion should engage in 10 seconds," Nick said, "if it doesn't overload and blow out both systems."

"I'm activating the automatic throttle," Cheeky said. "Let's keep our fingers crossed."

They raced back to the wrecker as the Corvette took off, speeding down the highway at two hundred miles an hour. They climbed in the truck and peered out the windshield just in time to see their makeshift spacecraft disappear into the midnight blue sky.

"Bunky doughnuts. Dough—nuts. Sounds interesting," Antage said, licking his lips. "How long until we reach our nearest convenient location?"

"Wait a minute," Avith said, punching a couple of controls on his console. "A smaller spacecraft has just left the planet's surface 45 kilometers west of the shuttle launch site. It's headed due east." Antage scowled at his computer screen.

"Identify the spacecraft and scan for life form readings," he barked. Avith quickly accessed the vast Galactic database.

"The vehicle is a 1999 Chevrolet Corvette — whatever that is — and there are two life forms aboard."

"Two life forms?"

"He is accused of Capital Murder," Avith pointed out. "Maybe he's taken a hostage."

"That's got to be it!" the senior Nebo said, taking firm hold of his control column. "Computer, switch to manual navigation." He glanced at his partner and sneered. "Let's nail that Selrahcian nebula scum!"

Chapter 16

CHEEKY STOMPED ON the gas pedal, tires scrunched gravel and the tow truck barreled across the parking lot, through the gate and back into the junkyard. He slammed on the brakes, spun the wheel and the wrecker fishtailed to a stop a few feet from the starcraft.

"Next stop Ohilabama bloody IV."

Nick bolted out of the truck and over to the ship to find me sitting in the co-pilot's seat, patiently awaiting his return. Two small leather suitcases sat side by side on the deck in the forward cabin area directly behind my chair.

"We need to get going," I said, strapping myself in with a sharp snap of my shoulder harness buckle. It was Nick's turn to arch an eyebrow at me.

"We?"

"Yes, I've decided to come along and help out with all this trouble you've gotten yourself into." Nick attempted to protest but I just raised my hand and didn't allow him a chance to speak. "From the looks of things, you're gonna need all the help you can get and Bablona says I have a very logical and analytical mind."

"That is correct," Babs said, as if on cue. My Buddy! Nick glowered at his computer and then turned and looked to Cheeky for support.

"Don't look at me. We've already discussed it and I agree with Bablona — Leddie could be of tremendous value to you."

"But, but I —," Nick sputtered. That was all the rebuttal he could muster at the moment.

"I've made my decision and YOU'RE wasting valuable time." Nick again scowled at me, Bablona and Cheeky — in that order. "Besides," I said, "if it weren't for us, you'd still be stumbling around in the scrub out on 256-A." Nick once again looked to Cheeky to back him up.

"I've seen that face before — the boss has made up her mind."

"Think about it, Nick. What's the worst that could happen? After all is said and done with your trial, what's the first thing the Galactic Council's gonna do with a lowly Class-D being like me — from a problem planet no less?" "Problem Planet" was uttered with my usual tinge of disdain. Nick didn't need to speculate.

"They'll order you to be shipped back to Earth at once."

"Right, so if that's the only downside, let's get going."

Nick took one final pleading look at Cheeky who said, "I'm with her, guv. She could use a vacation." He raised his hands and shrugged. "She hasn't taken one in years."

"But this violates Galactic Policy," Nick stammered.

"Oh, please!" I huffed. "Since when has that been a problem for you?" His shoulders slumped. We lowly humans had him and he knew it. And he certainly didn't have time to argue. One thing's for sure, the Association doesn't give us Class-D beings enough credit.

Cheeky came over to my side of the spacecraft, leaned in under the open hatch and gave me a long, don't-want-to-let-go hug.

"I'll see you when you get back, sweetheart." His eyes were starting to well with tears. (The only other time I've ever seen your Dad cry was when your Mom shipped out to Kuwait for Operation Desert Storm.)

"Love, love, love ya Luv," he said, his voice cracking slightly.

"Same here, Cheeky." I choked back some tears of my own and managed a mischievous grin. "Don't worry. Bablona'll take care of us." I said, glancing over at Nick to see if my wisecrack would get a reaction.

"Huh," was his response. Cheeky wiped his eyes and walked stiff-legged around the front of the ship to where Nick was standing. He shook his hand.

"I don't suppose I'll be seeing you again," he said, forlorn. "Take care of Leddie and — take care of yourself."

"So long, guv," Nick said fondly. "As far as beings in this part of the galaxy are concerned, you're definitely Class-A to me."

"Thanks, and give those Galactic Council Bastards bloody hell!"

"I'll do my best."

Just then, Nick realized that something was wrong with this picture; something's missing. He glanced around. "Where are Nikki and Marlowe?"

"I don't know," I said, also looking around. "I did take some time earlier to say goodbye to them."

"Marlowe!" Nick called out. "Nikki!"

We waited, all eyes searching the six acres of back lot.

"I could try and round them up," Cheeky offered.

"No matter," Nick said, without conviction. "We'd better get going." He climbed aboard, strapped himself in and hit a switch on the control console. The twin hatches to the cockpit lowered simultaneously with a hydraulic whoosh as Cheeky backed away.

"So long, Babs!" he called out.

"Goodbye, Cheeky," the computer replied a half-second before the hatches clamped shut.

"Activate lift propulsion," Nick ordered.

"Affirmative, lift propulsion engaged."

The ship ascended about a hundred feet straight up at a slow, steady pace — the lift propulsion turbines sounding just like a summer Florida cloudburst. Nick closed his eyes and concentrated on his feline friends. The two descendants of the ancient world of Felinus 4 immediately received his brain wave transmission and sent him back a surprisingly strong telepathic signal.

We'll always be with you, Nick.

"And I'll never be without you," Nick whispered, his voice choked with emotion.

Be cool. Don't be no galactic fool, Nikki added.

I just stared at Nick without speaking. He opened his eyes and turned to his self-appointed co-pilot.

"I'm really gonna miss the kitty cats," he said. I didn't have any words of consolation to offer because I felt the same way. I merely placed my hand on top of his.

"I guess they wanted to say goodbye in their own special way." I said.

"Yeah, I guess so."

"The Enforcement Department craft has changed course to intercept the decoy vehicle," Bablona reported, jolting us back to business. No time for sentiment.

"Once we break orbit – compute an ultra-light speed course for the Delta-Tau Wormhole – en route to Ohilibama IV."

"Affirmative," the computer responded. "Leddie, it is good to have you aboard."

"Thanks, Babs."

Nick harumpfed and ordered Bablona to engage the primary fusion thrusters.

"Fusion thrusters firing."

The ship blasted forward in a flash of blinding white-hot light. Eight-tenths of a second later, we were passing by Saturn.

"We'll intercept the renegade craft in twenty seconds," Avith said. He disengaged the fusion propulsion system and slowed the ED ship to intercept speed.

"Something's wrong," Antage said, puzzled. "That piece of shit spacecraft barely has enough power to make orbit. There's no way it could come close to reaching ultra-light speeds." The senior assistant popped a couple of keys on his computer and frowned at the screen.

"It also has a crude neutron field protecting the hull integrity and life support environment," Avith added.

Antage was getting a very bad feeling about this. It was inconceivable that the craft limping along ahead of them had interstellar capability. But, where in Zadar's name was Nek-Hånån's departmental ship?

"Subatomic matter is decaying on Krgobb. Let's run that piece of space junk down!"

"You got it," Avith said, "Intercept in ten seconds. Engaging tractor beam." The galactic starcraft easily overtook its target and its powerful tractor beam lassoed the sportscar-turned-spacecraft.

"Opening cargo bay doors," Antage informed his partner. In Avith's skilled hands, the Corvette was deftly guided into the ED craft and gently deposited in the middle of the cargo area. A high-pitched creak of the 'Vette's worn suspension reverberated through-out the empty bay as it touched down on the deck. Avith flipped a switch on his console and neutralized the neutron field and unlocked the car doors.

By now, Biff and Chili were wide-awake, pounding on the win-dows, half-crazed with fear, shock and, most of all, lack of brew.

"Get us the hell outta here!" Biff growled, punching the wind-shield with the back of his fist. Antage marched into the cargo area, approached the Corvette and casually opened the driver's side door. One look at the face of the noisier of his two captives told him that he and his partner had made a supernova-sized mistake.

"Who the hell are you!" Biff demanded, eyeing Antage's Enforcement Department uniform (which were surprisingly similar to uniforms worn by the Monorail attendants at Walt Disney World). "The Commander of Space Mountain?"

Chili, who had managed to extricate himself from the passenger seat, propped his elbows up on the roof and rubbed his throbbing temples. The burly Nebo-Jaasuian squared off in front of them, with arms folded and face grimacing. This was not gonna look good back at Galactic Regional.

"These guys sure ain't from the government — not our govern-ment anyway," Chili said, recalling their encounter with Nick and Cheeky.

"No shit, Shirley," Biff snarled. He was quickly overcoming the disorientation caused by all that he and his little brother had been through since arriving at Salvage Specialists earlier that evening.

"I'm Antage Lotan of the Galactic Association of Star System's Enforcement Department." Avith arrived in time to hear his part-ner's introduction and stood next to him, joining in on the folded arms, face grimacing routine. They looked like a pair of very large, interplanetary humanoid bookends.

"And I'm his partner, Avith Skairac."

An exhausted Biff slumped against the sportscar's rear fender, shaking his head and looking around the cargo bay. "You guys wouldn't happen to have any beer on this thing, would you?"

Chapter 17

PROVIDING THE ONLY source of light inside the cockpit of Nick's starship were the computer screens, readout displays and hundreds of multi-colored indicator lamps lining the control consoles. We were only hours into our flight, but already millions of miles from Earth's solar system speeding towards the Delta Tau Wormhole.

Once transversed, the Delta Tau would spew our ship out a mere eleven light years from Ohilibama IV and our secret rendezvous with Merek.

I was curled up, half asleep in the co-pilot's seat, exhausted after the excitement of the past few days. I peeked out under one eyelid to see Nick slump down in the command chair, ready to surrender to the tranquility of sleep, safe in the knowledge that Bablona's course program was handling the ship's navigation.

His eyes strayed from the mesmerizing panorama of stars racing by on the front viewscreen to my sleep-contorted face. (I'm just glad I wasn't doing something gross — like drooling out of the side of my mouth.) Although he initially objected to me accompanying him, deep down I knew he was glad I had insisted on coming along.

"Babs, do you think it was a good idea to bring Leddie?"

"Given her strong will and stubborn nature, I do not believe you were in a position to decline."

"Strong-willed and stubborn, but at the same time, bossy."

I'm gonna remember that crack, buster.

"Precisely."

"But what about her Class-D designation?"

"Perhaps you can request a status upgrade." My pal, Babs.

"You know, that's not a bad idea. Sometimes Merek can work wonders with Galactic Regional."

About thirty thousand more stars whizzed by when the peace and quiet was disturbed by a strange rumbling sound coming from inside one of the cargo holds astern. Nick sprang up from his chair.

"Holy Cow! What was that?"

"Internal sensors indicate two life forms located in the right rear cargo hold," Bablona informed him. The unidentified rustling also stirred me from my semi-comatose slumber. I jumped up in my seat with a start.

"What's the matter? What's going on?"

"Something's making noise in the rear compartment."

"Really?"

"Can you identify these life forms?" Nick asked the computer.

"Did you say life forms?" I said, sitting up and rubbing the sleep from my eyes. Confusion quickly turned to suspicion. "Wait a minute — I've got a funny feeling I know exactly who these life forms are!"

"The life forms are identified as Nikki and Marlowe," Babs replied. The handle on the cargo hold door clicked several times and the hatch fell open spilling two fluff-laden stowaways out onto the deck. They landed on their paws (of course) and casually strolled toward the cockpit.

Hey, how's it going? Marlowe relayed, attempting the casual approach.

"No wonder your farewell thought transmission was coming in so strong!" Nick realized aloud.

Hey, nice spacecraft, Nikki brain-waved, sauntering up to my chair.

"How did you guys get in there?" I asked sternly. Both kitties switched to their "too cute for words" mode and four feline eyes trained on me adoringly. They began purring and rubbing against my legs, really doing up the affection routine.

Really nice ship, Nick, Marlowe reiterated, trying to change the subject.

Yeah, way cool, Nikki concurred, peering up at the viewscreen. *Was that the Orion Nebula we just passed?* Nick curtly addressed Bablona.

"Did you know these two were on the ship?"

"Affirmative. My sensors identified their life signs as soon as they boarded." Nick glanced at me and then back to Babs.

"If you knew they were on board, why didn't you report it?" Babs' blue lights stared at Nick for precisely 6.17 seconds.

"You did not request that information."

Nikki and Marlowe sat side by side on the deck, with smug looks on their snouts, thoroughly enjoying the exchange between Nick and the computer.

There's not much they can do at this point, Marlowe relayed to his little sister.

Yeah, what are they gonna do? Nikki agreed. *Turn around and take us back?* I shot my Himalayan a reproachful glare.

"I'll bet you're behind this, you big stinker!" Marlowe's blue eyes squeezed shut smugly.

Actually, it was Nikki's idea.

"Dammit to hell! I wish there was some way I could understand what these two little creepazoids were thinking!" I scowled at my kitty cats who just feigned nonchalance. Nick smirked.

"It just so happens that I was gonna talk to you about that before we reached Ohilibama IV."

"Oh?"

The alien walked back to a console directly across from the cargo hold. "If you expect to be of any assistance to me, you're gonna have to understand what's being said." He activated a couple of controls and a narrow metal drawer opened. He removed a large, needleless syringe-like device. "This is the ship's medical station. I was gonna suggest we implant a translator module into your brain — it'll work like those interpreter devices they use at the United Nations." I eyed the syringe warily, noting with only a small measure of relief that there was no sharp needle of proportionate size attached to it. "However," Nick continued, "instead of translating only a handful of languages, this module can decode thousands of verbal and nonverbal forms of communication from cultures throughout the Association."

"Will it hurt?"

Nick stepped over to me, stuck the syringe directly behind my right ear and squeezed.

"It won't hurt a bit," he said in his native Selrahcian tongue. My face lit up.

"This is great! I understood you as if you were speaking English!"

"Precisely. Welcome to the rest of the galaxy." My smile immediately disappeared and I turned toward the two stowaways.

Uh-oh! the felines brain-waved.

"Uh-oh," is right you two." The kitty cats once again attempted to distract me by purring and rubbing against my legs.

We just wanted to be with you! Marlowe relayed, flashing his trademark blue eyes affectionately.

"Oh, please!" I huffed, "and don't think this lovey-dovey routine is going to get you two out of the doghouse."

DOG-house? The cats gaped at each other with eyes bulged wide. *How repulsive!*

Chapter 18

CHEEKY HAD JUST popped the top off the last remaining Guinness Stout when he heard a strange, turbulent "whooshing" sound coming from directly above the showroom building. He ran out into the parking lot in time to see the Corvette being deposited in the middle of State Road 256-A by a neon violet beam of light emanating from a dark gray spacecraft hovering overhead. It was bigger than Nick's ship — same charcoal color — with perhaps a little sportier styling.

"They're using a tractor beam — too bloody cool!" The 'Vette's frame and suspension creaked loudly again as the car touched down on the pavement. "I've got to do something about that damn suspension system," he said, scratching his head. The purple light terminated and the spacecraft vanished.

Cheeky gazed up at the now-vacant sky. The ED boys, as Nick called them, must have calculated the decoy's flight trajectory and returned it to its original liftoff coordinates.

He approached the Corvette cautiously and both doors flew open. Dazed and confused (for once, not due to any alcoholic stimuli), Biff and Chili Breeto stumbled out of the sportcar's low slung frame. They spotted Cheeky marching towards them and bolted for Chili's battered old Monte Carlo which was still parked in the junkyard lot. Cheeky grinned and called out to the pair of unlikely astronauts. They paid him no mind. With arms and elbows pumping, the big redneck and his little brother sprinted across the parking lot and dived into the vintage '87 Chevrolet rustbucket. Chili frantically cranked the key in the ignition and, after a couple of internal combustion burps, the engine reluctantly fired up, exhaling a big cloud of black smoke. The Monte Carlo roared out of the lot, the remnants of its tattered vinyl roof flapping in the breeze.

Cheeky stood on the gravel, grinning as he shook his head and watched the car disappear down the highway. He then fetched the tow truck, hauled the Corvette back through the chained link fence and stowed it in the utility shed.

— — —

Fourteen days, fifteen hours and sixteen minutes into our space flight, my romantic vision of traveling to strange new worlds in distant parts of the galaxy had paled considerably. Crimony sakes! In all those science fiction movies, intrepid spacefarers could traverse thousands of light years, save entire solar systems, and return to Earth all in an hour and forty-five minutes. In the real universe, I was finding out, the Space-Time Continuum could be a real pain in the ass.

The kitty cats seemed unaffected by the situation. They spent most of their time as they would if they were back home — they slept.   For them, the cool surface of the starcraft's aft deck was the perfect place to stretch out and catch some "Z's."

Nikki and Marlowe seemed to have a unique ability to adapt to these incredible circumstances all too easily. Maybe there was something to Nick's incredible story about them being descendants of an ancient planet light years and centuries from present-day Earth.

I was still a little peeved at the two of them for tagging along, but what could I do at this point? Besides, I relished the ability, thanks to the translator module, of knowing exactly what those two little stinkers were up to!

I passed the endless hours reviewing Bablona's Galactic Law and History files and watching movies in Nick's film collection. His taste in cinema was eclectic at best — Hollywood classics, Bogart films, Marx Brothers comedies (I didn't see what was so funny about them), and some weird, yet interesting, offering from other planets. These "foreign" films were also especially entertaining to me because I could now understand the dialogue, if not all the extraterrestrial symbolism. I was also very impressed with the Goganian cinema verté filmed in 360 degrees and viewed with a virtual reality style helmet. It was like you were actually a character in the movie. Nick said these films were popular with galactic movie buffs throughout the Association, even though they were a cinematic nightmare for directors to film and edit.

As captivating as the film library was, I found Bablona's history files were even more fascinating — they told the story of the Galactic Association of Star Systems.

Fifty millennia ago, Procyon II's leading astrophysicist, Zadar Ko, designed and constructed a prototype starcraft as part of her eighth doctoral thesis: "The Space-Time Continuum: What's In It For Us?"

Little did Zadar realize, when she squeezed her diminutive physique into the cramped cockpit of the experimental craft, that she was about to embark on a journey that would eventually lead to the formation of an association of planets that would stretch halfway across the galaxy.

A quiet and unassuming professor of astrophysics and fusion propulsion at Procyon A&M (Aeronautic and Mass-Energy Relations) University, Zadar Ko was known more for her academic and scholastic achievements. But, her revolutionary innovations in directed laser propulsion and ramscoop hull design led to the construction of an interstellar spacecraft that could achieve and maintain speeds of up to .9 light speed.

Zadar's reactor prototype had the ability to harness incredible amounts of energy produced by a fusion reaction utilizing a combination of Iridium and a Procyon isotope called Caladonium. This energy was then directed into a particle accelerator that produced a matter-anti-matter reaction.

In an early test, the awesome power generated by this experimental reactor prototype completely obliterated Hoobb, fifteenth and furthest of Procyon IX's moons. When Zadar focused the matter-anti-matter energy into a concentrated laser beam, it created a subspace field which severely curved the fabric of space-time, allowing the prototype starcraft to achieve near light speed.

Armed with only her resolve and quantum discs containing 30,000 hours of her favorite soap opera, Galactic Hospital ("GH" as it was known to its fans), Zadar left Procyon II and headed for the Pyxis Star System in hopes of achieving her lifelong goal: contact with another planetary species.

Zadar spent the next hundred and fifty years hurtling through the black void of space in the tiny single-occupant spacecraft.

Finally, just when she was really getting sick of GH "reruns," SFAOT (Search For Anybody Out There) astronomers from the highly advanced and incredibly fashionable planet of Pyxis III picked up the faint energy signature emanating from Zadar's ship on their long-range sensors.

Up to this point, the Pyxis had developed safe and reliable interplanetary space travel and had extensively explored their twelve-world solar system. They had also recently discovered the first stable wormhole just outside the orbital path of Pyxis XII, the outermost planet in their system.

Development of a craft with interstellar capability, however, had been delayed by lack of progress in astropropulsion technology and a long run of extremely successful resort and theater seasons.

For almost a year, the Pyxis scientists tracked the mysterious spacecraft while snacking on stuffed mushrooms, Alterian Brie and sipping a very amusing Nebelan Blanc. Finally, just as a very successful all-night "first contact" party was starting to get dull, Zadar's tiny ship triumphantly entered orbit around Pyxis III.

Although most of them were nursing pulsar-sized hangovers, the leaders of the Pyxis scientific community were amazed by Zadar's advanced propulsion designs and immediately suggested they combine their research towards enhancing the capabilities of her prototype. Pyxis physicists hit on the idea of adding a substance called Catatonium 11-13 to the fusion reaction in combination with the Iridium and Caladonium. The result was a regenerating energy source which, when focused into Zadar's matter-anti-matter laser propulsion system, produced extremely high quantities of tachyon particles.

Thought to exist in theory only, tachyon particles are subatomic particles that move faster than the speed of light.

The era of ultra-light speed travel had dawned. Within a few short years, it would be possible to venture out into the far reaches of galactic space.

The Pyxis, much to their surprise and personal satisfaction, were also successful in providing the bookwormish and self-conscious Zadar with extensive instruction in Cooliousity (the art of being "Cool"), revamping what they considered a drab, frumpish wardrobe and getting rid of her "godawful" bangs.

Lance Ramalamadingdong (no kidding), the universally recognized leader of Pyxis society and the person considered to be the coolest, hippest being in the galaxy, much to everyone's utter amazement, immediately became enamored with the brilliant, but painfully shy, Procyon scientist.

Lance was the owner and chief operating officer of the Pyxis Corporation, a company that specialized in the design and manufacture of personal interplanetary spacecraft — Pyxis III's leading growth industry.

Zadar reciprocated Lance's feelings of affection and the two soon became inseparable. (Down through the ages, their great love story has been immortalized in numerous literary, theatrical and cinematic works. Among the most famous were: "A Starcraft Named Desire," "The Last Time I Saw Parvek," and the Galactic Film Academy award-winning GoGanian 360-film, "On A Clear Day You Can See For Light Years.")

Inspired by his beloved's achievements in astropropulsion, Lance began to formulate theories on how to make exploration of interstellar space feasible. According to him, war and aggression were inefficient and cost-prohibitive means to venture out into a galaxy 100 thousand light years in size. He felt that an organization of planets, bound together by a comprehensive, codified set of operating policies and procedures, was the only efficient means of reaching out to the stars.

Expansion on a much larger scale came with the discovery of the Kappa Kegga Wormhole, which led to contact with the technically advanced and sociologically enlightened inhabitants of Ohilibama IV.

Although the "too-cool" Pyxis considered the studious and scholarly Ohilibamans a tad dry for their taste (and very dull at cocktail parties), they were nonetheless extremely impressed with their achievements in inertia theory, particle physics and quantum mechanics.

Ohilibama IV provided the vital third leg of the Procyon-Pyxis-Ohilibama triangle and an interplanetary alliance was formed. This alliance was the predecessor to the Galactic Association of Star Systems (GASS).

Selrahc, parenthetically, was not accepted into the Association until a couple of millennia later, the Tegl-va situation relegating them to problem-planet status. It was only because of Selrahc's close proximity to the Beta-Gamma Wormhole, a major galactic crossroads, that the planet was reluctantly granted admittance.

"So, Mr. Advanced Galactic Being," I said out of the side of my mouth to Marlowe, "the only reason your planet even got into the Association was because of favorable geographic circumstance."

And this comes as a surprise to you? Marlowe relayed before rolling over on his other side and going back to sleep.

This particularly intensive viewing session left me tired and a little grumpy. I wearily trudged back to the cockpit and I plopped down in the co-pilot's chair.

"Nick." My plaintive whine was reminiscent of a small child, stuck in the back seat of the family station wagon for the better part of a two-week summer vacation. I felt like saying: When are we there? What I actually asked was: "How long until we reach the wormhole?"

Nick pointed to a small, barely discernible patch of black starless space, dead ahead.

"THAT is the Delta Tau Wormhole," he announced, as if he had personally discovered it. "It'll transport us to the Ohilibama Star System – hundreds of light years across this sector of space – in about nine-and-a-half minutes."

A cold chill ran down my spine. Suddenly, the thought of being so far from home frightened me. Maybe this "vacation" wasn't such a good idea after all.

"Better strap in," Nick cautioned, pulling his shoulder harness taut across his body. I immediately did as he said.

"What about the kitty cats?"

"They'll be fine. They always land on their feet, don't they?" Nikki and Marlowe heard their cue and, from a sound sleep, popped their heads up. How they did this always mystified me.

Always land on our PAWS! the big Himalayan corrected Nick. He got up, sauntered over to my seat, and promptly hopped into my lap.

"Ouff!" I wheezed. "Marlowe, you need to go on a diet."

I'm not fat, he relayed, indignant. *I'm just incredibly fluffy.*

"Yeah, right, Mr. Fifteen Pounds and counting."

What's going on? Nikki wondered, bouncing up into Nick's lap and resting her front paws on the control column. (Fortunately, the ship's automatic navigation was engaged.) Both she and her big brother stared out the viewscreen.

"We have just entered the Delta Tau Wormhole," Bablona reported.

The ship blazed forward, instantaneously accelerating to one hundred times its previous ultra-light velocity. The millions of stars on the viewscreen stretched into infinite bands of elongated blinding light, the colors of which spanned the entire visual spectrum.

Nick, the kitties and I were slammed back into our seats by the intense Z-forces (G-forces, cubed) created by the wormhole's skewed spatial plane. Our eyes bulged, our jaws flew open at contorted angles and our skulls felt like they were going to implode. Bablona increased power to the Internal Environment Subsystem, but we could still feel the effects of the tremendous forward thrust inside the cockpit.

The sudden, severe increase in momentum taxed the life support and inertial systems to their limits as kaleidoscopic bands of yellow, red, green, blue and violet flashed by like raging white water around a submerged raft. (Dispersion scans indicate we have just passed through a metaphoric anomaly).

Nikki and Marlowe dug their claws into our pant legs, drawing blood, but Nick and I were too busy death-gripping our chair arms to notice.

The physical laws of normal fourth dimensional space-time became moot and vast stretches of interstellar space were traversed in milliseconds as the starcraft attained speeds that rendered everything on the viewscreen a hot-pink (or fuchsia, if you will) blur.

We had to shield our eyes from the blinding display of distorted space and time blazing by on the viewer as the ship achieved unfathomable velocities, now thousands of times faster than the speed of light. The outer hull creaked and swayed under the unrelenting pressure as it buffeted against the contorted geometric plane of the wormhole's hypersurface but Bablona, amazingly, managed to keep the ship on course.

Precisely 9.23 minutes after entering the wormhole, the ship abruptly lurched back into normal space. The automatic breaking thrusters fired and used a full light year's distance to slow the craft to mere ultra-light velocity in order to prevent the hull from breaching and the ship and everyone aboard from exploding into billions and billions of subatomic particles.

We were now thirty-five hundred light years from where we had entered the wormhole.

"Exiting the Delta Tau Wormhole," Bablona informed us. "Two point one seven hours to the Ohilibama Star System."

Chapter 19

"NEK-HÅNÅN! YOU sorry son of a dwarf star!" Merek called out from the top step of the Galactic Law Library located in Erq, the largest city on Ohilibama IV.

The planet of Ohilibama IV was one of the most advanced and impressive charter members of the Galactic Association of Star Systems. Geographically similar to Earth, the planet had four huge salt water oceans and seven continents. Unlike Earth, the majority of its land mass was located near the equator — the renowned Rain Forests of Ohilibama.

Unmolested by the planet's inhabitants, the millions of acres of lush tropical woodlands provided the necessary hydrogen, oxygen and nitrogen to sustain carbon-based life. The rain forests produced these elements in abundant quantity along with another substance known as anthrogen. This curious element, found on only a handful of worlds in the known galaxy, reacted synergistically with Ohilibaman DNA to prevent insecurity and low self-esteem. Because of this, the Ohilibamans, who physically resembled the aliens described in all those Earth UFO encounter stories — slight of body, three feet tall, with oversized teardrop heads and almond-shaped eyes — were able to build a planet-wide society known for its intellectual and galactarian achievements. Culturally, sociologically and scientifically, Ohilibama IV, or "Bama" as it was called, was the center star in the Association's ring nebula.

The ultra-modern metropolis of Erq featured the quadrant's largest, busiest and most efficient starport, handling thousands of arriving and departing starcraft daily and hardly ever losing any luggage.

Merek grasped his subordinate by the right shoulder after Nick, the kitty cats and I had trudged up what seemed like a thousand midnight-blue brick steps that lead to the library's grandiose pillared entrance. The two exchanged the traditional Selrahcian greeting — right hand balled in a fist, brushed lightly against the other's cheek. I thought the gesture reminiscent of the old black-and-white Hollywood movies where one character feigned socking the other on the jaw and hoped to hell it wasn't some type of galactic male bonding thing.

Velitel, fellow native of Nick's home world, followed with the same greeting.

"Good to see you again, Ithran," he said, glancing over at me.

"We call him Nick," I blurted out, stepping forward and speaking up a tad too quickly. Sorry, but meeting alien beings from other parts of the galaxy was not one of my regular activities. "It's easier to pronounce," I nervously explained. Merek and Velitel turned their attention away from Nick and toward the obviously self-conscious stranger — me.

"I'll have to go along with you on that one," Merek said, flashing a warm smile. "I've always had trouble with Selrahcian names."

"Leddie Fennhadden," I said with increased confidence, extending my right hand out of habit. Merek and Velitel's congenial and easy-going manner had instantly made me feel at ease.

"My pleasure. I'm Merek," the large Beoran said, realizing instinctively that he should grasp my outstretched hand. Making strangers feel welcome came naturally to him — he was considered one of the most charming beings in the galaxy. In fact, everyone from Merek's home world, Beor, was charming.

Neither aggressive nor militant by nature, the Beoran species evolved highly developed interpersonal communication skills. Unlike many worlds, their planet's history was not plagued by centuries of aggression, war and military conquest. On the contrary, Beor's various cultures fostered peaceful relations with one another through negotiation, compromise and mutually satisfactory accord. Their serene global environment and position as one of the most respected worlds in the Association was a direct result of this peaceful heritage. In addition, the Beoran species was blessed with a wonderful sense of humor.

This single character trait ultimately proved to be the planet's salvation.

Two millennia ago, the warrior race, the Congengabians, made the initial interstellar contact with the remote Beoran star system. An intelligent, bipedal reptilian race, Congengabians were a hostile and aggressive species who lived and died by the positron laser. They had conquered several neighboring star systems by force, and made no secret of their intention to expand their power and control throughout the galaxy by any means necessary.

A huge convoy of heavily-armed Congengabian starcruisers entered Beoran space, ready, willing and able to prey on the smaller and weaker. The Beorans, no match strategically for the invaders, turned to their greatest single asset as a species to save their world from destruction.

They turned on the charm.

Like a small, but quick-witted child using a clever quip to preclude a beating at the hands of a schoolyard bully, the Beorans concentrated their efforts to making the ominous visitors laugh like hell. (It was also extremely fortunate for their cause that the arrival of the Congengabian fleet coincided with the 3951st Annual Beoran Comedy Festival.) The Congengabians were so impressed with the humor and gracious nature of the Beorans that THEY suggested forming an alliance — an alliance that has survived to the present day.

"And this is my cohort and legal advisor, Azor-Zadok Velitel," Merek announced, introducing his long-time companion. The galactic lawyer extended his hand towards me, imitating my gesture.

"Charmed," he drawled. "Leddie Fen —,"

"Fennhadden," I spouted. Velitel chuckled.

"Somebody said something about Selrahcian names being difficult?"

I couldn't help but like these two — they were so personable. Their charm was especially appealing when I considered the average Salvage Specialist customer made Biff Breeto look like Cary Grant.

Ah — excuse me; aren't you forgetting somebody? Marlowe relayed, annoyed that he wasn't getting enough attention. Merek leaned over, hands on knees and addressed the kitty cats.

"And who do we have here?"

I'm Marlowe and this is my little sister, Nikki, the big cat brainwaved with the utmost confidence. *We're descendants of the ancient world of Felinus 4.*

How's it going? Nikki communicated, her pretty emerald eyes trained on the portly Beoran.

"Sister and brother, eh? Well, it's a pleasure to meet you both," Merek said. "On my home world, we value family above all else. I don't know what I'd do without my siblings — all sixty-five of them." Four feline eyes widened with surprise upon hearing the prodigious number in Merek's family unit.

Worse than Catholics, Nikki observed.

"And I'm the runt of the litter!" Merek added. The kitties gaped at each other.

I'll bet you go through a lot of tuna, Marlowe chimed in telepathically.

"Speaking of tuna – is anybody hungry?" Velitel asked everyone.

I'm starving!" Marlowe responded without the slightest hesitation.

"Well, that's a shocker," I deadpanned, receiving a pickle puss from him for my remark. Merek patted his ample stomach with both hands.

"I'm with Marlowe. I could use a bite to eat."

"How about Galacto-Burger?" Velitel suggested.

"Excellent!" His portly companion said, enthusiastically seconding the motion. Everyone turned around and promptly headed back down the dark brick steps.

"Burgers?" I caught Nick by the arm. "I thought you said these two were food connoisseurs."

"Leddie," Nick explained patiently, "a meal consisting of some type of protein compound, served between two pieces of yeast-rising carbohydrate, is a galactic staple."

"Oh, well, since you've made it sound so yummy," I said, trailing behind the rest of the group and, once again, shaking my head in disbelief.

From the Law Library, we would proceed to the hydro-tram that would take us to the starport and Nick's ship.

"Besides Leddie, you haven't lived until you've tasted a Galacto-Burger!"

— — —

"It is a pleasure to have you aboard," Bablona 66-L told Merek and Velitel as the spacecraft broke orbit and headed for Oniram, the largest of Ohilibama's seven moons.

"We'll get something to eat and discuss the case over dinner," Merek said, appointing himself the group's activities coordinator.

Do they have tuna? Marlowe inquired anxiously. The lawyer flashed the big kitty a sly grin.

"I'll be willing to bet you'll forget all about tuna after tasting some Alterian Albacore."

Hmmm — sounds interesting.

"I can't believe they have fast food out here in space." I was still operating in a perpetual state of mild shock, given all I had seen and heard since leaving dear old Mother Earth.

"Well, Leddie," Nick said, pointing towards the viewscreen, "Check it out." The cats and I stared at the viewer, transfixed by the awe-inspiring sight of a gigantic cylindrical space station in orbit around Oniram. It revolved slowly on its axis as thousands of interior lights sparkled against the black backdrop of deep space. A fuchsia neon sign, several stories high, blinked on and off, identifying the spaceborne structure as the GALACTO-BURGER FLY-IN RESTAURANT.

As our ship made its initial approach, we could see strange starcraft from all over the quadrant arriving and departing from a myriad of docking bays located around the station's circumference. Chuck Berry's "Little Queenie" blasted over Babs' comm-speaker originating from the Galacto-Burger's custom Giggawatt sound system. I wrinkled my nose.

"Isn't that — ?"

"Chuck Berry." Merek said, immediately identifying the Rock and Roll legend.

"Great stuff, isn't it?" Velitel said, bobbing his head to the beat.

"Yeah, it's great — but how do you guys know about him? Merek and Velitel mugged and shrugged at each other.

"Do you remember the NASA probe, Voyager?" Merek asked. I gave a slight nod, acknowledging a vague familiarity with the name of the unmanned spacecraft. "It was launched from Earth decades ago on a mission to explore your solar system. From there, it was programmed to continue out into space in hopes of making contact with — well, us."

"Included in the probe's data banks was information about Earth and its neighboring planets," Velitel said. "It also contained renderings of the male and female human form, greetings in several Earth languages and music from different eras of your planet's history."

"It had everything from Bach to Beethoven," Merek added. "Bernstein to Berry."

"Yeah, okay — I seem to remember reading something about that," I said. "So?"

"The Chuck Berry music was the only material included in Voyager's databanks that interested us."

"We had Nick send us his entire collection," Merek said. "In fact, Berry's classic double album, 'The Great 28,' took over the top spot on the Galactic Music Charts and has stayed number one for the past three decades."

The previous number one recording was the "Symphony Erotica in R-Flat Minor" by the reknowned Goganian composer, Pazh Hzap. This symphony was purported to cause sexual arousal among many of the species inhabiting the known galaxy.

It remained at the top of the charts for nearly three centuries.

"Chuck Berry's music has a very unusual and interesting syncopation — very stimulating," Velitel observed.

'Yeah, yeah, I know," I groaned, anticipating the well-worn cliché. "And it's great to dance to."

"Dance to?" Merek glanced over at Velitel. "We never thought of that."

I slumped down in my seat and stared out at the Galacto-Burger. It certainly is strange out here in galactic space.

Nick slowed the craft to approach speed, took a wide arcing course, and deftly pulled behind a bulbous gold and silver starship with wide windows that wrapped all the way around its hull. Inside, two five-foot long yellow-and-blue-striped fish were piloting craft amidst a transparent, liquid-filled environment. Their order: plankton-salad sandwiches — no beverage — was served through a pressurized hatch on the ship's starboard side.

Nikki and Marlowe stared out the viewer at the large aquatic species, licking their whiskers and pawing the surface of the screen.

Merek noticed the felines' keen interest.

"Those two are from the ocean planet of Binarius IX, an underwater world where the highest forms of life live under the sea."

Like Earth, Nikki relayed. I scrinched my nose at her.

"Earth?"

Yeah, Marlowe responded like the class know-it-all. *Dolphins, whales, felines — then humans, remember?* I sighed and rubbed my temples. They were starting to throb. And to think I actually insisted on coming along on this — "vacation."

The Binarius craft slipped out into space and Nick maneuvered the ship into the now-vacant spacedock.

"May I take your order?" the Galacto-Burger comm-system asked with perfect clarity.

Chapter
20

I TOOK A tentative first bite of my All-Galactic Burger with cheese, not sure of what to expect. It was at least a half-pound slab of some type of ground meat, grilled to perfection: charred black outside, pink and moist inside. I chewed slowly, at first, like a fussy child being introduced to the strange world of broccoli and cauliflower.

It was the most extraordinary taste I had ever experienced.

"Nick." I poked him in the ribs with my elbow. "This is terrific!" Nick finished a long pull off his GoGanian Lager and placed the amber bottle (with the distinctive zero-gravity pressurized cap) back down on the galley table.

"Ground Bekkan Woolly Mammoth makes the best burgers," he said, seizing his sandwich with both hands and taking a big bite. Since my mouth was full of food, I could only offer a concurring bob of my head.

With Bablona manning the helm, the starship maintained an orbit around Oniram's polar ice cap while we ate dinner and attempted to sort out Nick's defense strategy.

"As far as appearing before the Council is concerned," Velitel said, glancing around the table at us, "Nikki and Marlowe are no problem. Their Felinus 4 legacy confers upon them Class-B Galactic Status."

The kitty cats were oblivious to this part of the conversation. They were on the deck in front of the galley table chowing down on broiled Albacore and lapping up Kreggorian goat's milk. The lawyer took a sip of Xoian Ale. "However, the Council will not look favorably upon Leddie's presence — Class-D species designation, of course." Merek swallowed some of his Vegan Mondo Beast-Texas-Chili-Cheese Burger and shrugged.

"Not a problem. We'll just dress her in Beoran clothes and introduce her as my administrative assistant."

"How about Assistant Vice-President?" I suggested.

"All the better — and these days, pretty much the same thing anyway."

He took a healthy slug of Mahoogalian Indigo Ale and dabbed blue foam from his mouth and chin with his napkin.

"Besides, the Council will be too busy with the business at hand to pay much attention to her. Would anybody like some curly fries?"

One by one, we all shook our heads.

"The way I see the situation," Velitel said in between bites of Congengabian Barbeque, "the policy violations are obviously of secondary importance in comparison to the murder charge." (Lawyer talk is lawyer talk in all parts of the known galaxy.) "Nick's acts of planetary interference were of so little consequence — galactically speaking — that it's hard to believe they're gonna make a big issue of them."

I nearly choked on my pickle spear. Saving the Tribe of Israel? Sending Jesus, Mohammed and Buddha to save the souls of the human race? Jumpin' Jupiter! I'd hate to see what these galactic beings consider serious.

"Zadar's Radar!" Merek griped. "If they prosecuted every comparable interference violation, I'd have to haul half my department out of space and back to Regional — the Council would be booked solid through the next millennium!"

"I think we all agree that the Capital Murder charge is what they're going to try and hammer Nick on," the attorney said. "So we're gonna need some compelling and irrefutable evidence to support our defense."

"There's another factor that's gonna work against us," Merek said. "Regional Council nominations are coming up in less than two decades. The current members are all planning to run for reelection. They'll be looking to gain some notoriety from this very rare violent crime trial."

"That's a good point," Velitel agreed. "There's also gonna be some serious challenges to the existing members' re-election bids, which'll put these proceedings under even more intense scrutiny."

I sipped my beer. It was starting to sound like Nick's trial was more about politics than justice — like he was some sort of sacrificial lamb. I glanced at Nick, who was noticeably silent throughout this discussion. He only occasionally looked up from his burger (most of which remained uneaten) to offer a nervous nod of his head.

"Since Nick's with the Problem Planet Department, there'll be the usual debate over the policies concerning the addition of new worlds to the Association," Merek said, "but we've been hashing that issue out for centuries."

"What do you mean?" I asked.

"Many beings feel the continued expansion of GASS is not cost-effective," Velitel said.

"And the Problem Planet Department has always been a drag on the galactic profit margins," Merek added.

"Many beings feel it's better to just keep the size of the Association at its present level and divest itself of the planets currently in Merek's portfolio."

"Which'll eventually put my department out of business."

"But that's not fair," I protested. "It's not Earth's fault the Association won't accept us now."

"You're beginning to understand galactic corporate politics."

"I know for a fact," Merek said, "that Jidlaph and his cronies in Concurrence are always looking to cite my department over the most picayune policy violations."

"Tell me about it," Velitel groaned. "I'm always on the receiving end of your frantic thirty-ninth hour subspace transmissions."

"It's their way of telling us they consider Problem Planets a not-so-necessary evil."

I made a mental note to check the departmental profit and loss statements when I got back to the ship.

"Which brings us to the facts surrounding the alleged murder," the lawyer stated. "Okay, Nick, let's hear your side of the story."

"I can't tell you anything about it!" he snapped, suddenly becoming very upset. He was reacting just like he did back at the junk-yard. These requests for information, necessary for his defense, were really hitting a nerve. But why?

"What the hell's the matter with you? I said. "Is this why we came all the way out here? So that you can just give yourself up?"

Nick took a couple of stiff slugs off his beer.

"I promised I wouldn't reveal the identities of the others involved in the events in question. I'm sorry, but that's all I can say."

Merek and Velitel slouched back in their seats. Their worried looks began to betray doubts about Nick's innocence and a very long, very uncomfortable silence ensued. It was interrupted when Nick, much to everyone's surprise, asked if we might be able to negotiate some sort of plea bargain.

"It's a little premature for that, given we don't know how strong a case the prosecution has," the lawyer said, looking grim. "There also may not be much latitude to bargain with under current law. The maximum penalty the Council can impose for Capital Murder is immediate vaporization."

"Immediate vaporization!" I shrieked.

"I'm afraid he's correct," Nick said, staring into his beer bottle. "The Galactic Justice System doesn't allow capital crimes to go unpunished for decades while defendants file appeal after appeal – like in America."

"But isn't that a little severe?"

"Let's see." Merek placed his comm-unit on the table and punched a couple of buttons. "The statutory provision for the vaporization sentence is still on the books — dates back to GASS: 2309."

"2309 was the height of the Special Prosecutor Wars," Velitel said, shaking his head in disgust. "Perhaps the darkest chapter in Association history."

O—kay. I made another mental note to check the galactic history files when I got back to the ship.

"If the Council is willing to accept a plea," the lawyer speculated, "we might be able to negotiate a couple hundred years of galactic service — but I'm just guessing. And you'll be stripped of all your Association seniority and benefits."

"That's if they're even willing to consider a deal," Merek said, peering over his bifocals at Nick. "The serious nature of the crime isn't gonna work in our favor."

"Nor is the highly charged political climate," Velitel added, trying to sound as ominous as possible.

"That's why you've got to tell us everything you know about what happened," I pleaded, grabbing and squeezing his arm with both hands.

She's right – the more we know, the better we'll be able to defend you, Marlowe relayed only after finishing his dinner. Nick downed more beer but said nothing.

"Who is he accused of killing?" I asked, as if I would actually know the identity of the interstellar murder victim. Merek couldn't recall the name and had to consult his comm-unit.

"Let's see. His name was J. Fitzgerald Kennedy and he was some type of planetary head of state."

"J. Fitzgerald Kennedy. JOHN Fitzgerald KENNEDY! Holy Shit!" I slid off the galley bench and fell onto the deck, landing on what I considered my most well-padded feature.

She's friggy freakin'! Nikki relayed. Merek bolted up, rushed to my side and grabbed me by the arm. "Are you all right?" he asked, helping me back into my seat. For a big being, he was deceptively quick and agile.

"Can you give us any information about the victim?" the lawyer asked. This time, I gulped some beer.

"Well — he was the President — ah — the elected leader of the United States of America. That's the country on Earth where the cats and I live. I glanced over at Nick and an ice-cold shiver ran down my spine. "He was assassinated over forty years ago."

Merek and Velitel leaned forward in their chairs. The Beoran spoke first, addressing Nick.

"You know I think of you as more than just an employee. And you know we're here out of concern for your welfare.".

"We just want to help the best way we can," Velitel added.

"I can't tell you anything!" Nick snarled. "I made a promise!" With that, he snatched his beer and bolted up from his seat. He stalked over to the cockpit and gaped out the forward viewscreen at the ice-capped gray moon.

Something about this case was bothering me — a piece was missing and I couldn't figure out what it was.

Then it hit me.

Nick was protecting somebody, sacrificing himself to keep the others involved out of it. That's the key. But who else was involved — and how in Zadar's name was I gonna find them out here?

"Oh, my God!" I gasped under my breath, before I could catch myself.

"Did you say something?" Merek asked, now peering down his bifocals at me. "Nothing," I replied in little more than a whisper. Merek let it pass — for the time being. I gulped more beer and tried to chill out.

I needed to talk to Babs — alone!

"Well, there's not a lot we can do without more information," Velitel said, as he drained the last of his ale.

"I understand," Nick said, without turning his attention from the viewscreen. "And I appreciate you guys trying to help — but I can't break my promise." The kitty cats, their tummies now sufficiently full, sauntered over to Nick and rubbed against his legs, purring loudly.

It's okay, buddy, Nikki relayed. *We're with you all the way.*

Well, at least until they get to the vaporization part.

Marlowe! Nikki admonished her brother and then turned to Counsel. *Are there any planets that don't have an extradition treaty with the Association?* she asked telepathically. Merek and Velitel gaped at each other.

"That could be a temporary solution to the problem," the lawyer said. "I don't think the Congengabians ever negotiated an extradition agreement."

"That could buy us some time," Merek said. "But to what end?"

"If the consequences are immediate vaporization — any delay would be preferable," I pointed out.

"Merek, could you talk to your Congengabian contacts and see what might be feasible?" Velitel asked.

"Sure, can't hurt to ask."

Chuck Berry was halfway through the second chorus of "Oh Baby Doll" when the comm-system suddenly went dead. From out of nowhere, the image of the Enforcement Department starcraft appeared, filling the viewscreen and Antage Lotan's surly voice blared over the monitor: "I've got bad news for you, Azor — your ship is now under the control of our tractor beam. We'll be escorting you and everyone on board back to Regional Headquarters on Baltrus VII for trial."

Chapter 21

DESPITE OUR DESPERATE situation, I couldn't refrain from "oooing and aahing" (typical interstellar tourist behavior according to Babs) at the breathtaking sight that was the Galactic Regional Complex on Baltrus VII. I couldn't help it. I had never seen architecture so wondrous. The buildings were towering obtuse-angled glass and metal structures connected by arched promenades and pretty open-air piazzas. The meticulously landscaped grounds contained acres upon acres of all sorts of exotic plant life. There were these majestic alien Sequoias, vibrant with baby blue foliage and long rows of haunting black willows that lined beds of intricately shaped flowers in brilliant colors and hues I'd never seen before. I quickly stifled my enthusiasm after glancing over at a distraught and sullen Nick, trudging wearily towards his fateful date with the Regional Council.

The Enforcement Department craft's long-range scanners had been able to trace the tachyon particle residue left by Nick's ship after it left Earth's atmosphere and Avith extrapolated a starcourse that led straight to the Delta-Tau Wormhole. From there, it didn't take a Sherlock Holmes or a Sub-Inspector Da-Zeo (from GoGanius Alpha) to figure out that Ohilibama IV was our probable destination.

Antage and Avith, grim-faced and officious, herded Nick and the defense team, which now consisted of Velitel, Merek, me and the kitty cats, into the hydro-lift in front of the Council Hall. The lift ascended three stories in as many seconds and the ED assistants marched us across a purple-floored foyer and down a mirrored hallway that led into the Council Chambers.

I stumbled along, struggling in the crimson and orange (ugh!) Beoran robe Merek had provided for my disguise. The always-curious kitties were at my heels, snooping and sniffing everything within their sensor range.

Velitel motioned us to our seats behind the table designated for the defense and I gathered up the bulky garment and carefully sat down. Merek was used to the flowing style of his native dress, which hid his portly frame well, but for me, the alien garb was cumbersome. I did decide, upon further consideration, however, that it was a hell of a lot better than clomping around in pantyhose and heels. Talk about primitive!

We sat four abreast behind the thick black slab table while Nikki and Marlowe parked their hindquarters on the church pew-like bench directly behind us in the first row of the gallery. Two of the members of the Regional Council, Jidlaph and Uz, sat on high and stoically surveyed their lowly galactic minions. Only Kothan, the senior V.P., seemed to be respectful of our presence.

Although Kothan was a native of Moogalie, a planet whose culture was centered around superficial values and self-promotion, he was something of an enigma to his fellow Moogalies and to Pahoogalies like Jidlaph. The son of two Association ambassadors, Kothan spent his formative years traveling throughout the galaxy with his parents, spending summers quantum-golfing on Regulon V and fusion boarding on the Pyxis Pleasure Planet known as "The Hamptons." (Remember what's been said about coincidence.) Removed from the shallow value system of his home world, he developed into a well-respected leader known for his insightful and pragmatic nature. These character traits served him well throughout his one hundred and forty year tenure as Senior Vice President and head of the Regional Council.

"I see the defendant and his representatives have arrived," Kothan observed. "For the record, counsel, please identify the others present on behalf of the defendant."

This hearing, as with all formal Association proceedings, was being broadcast live via subspace transmission to billions of beings throughout the Association over GNN: The Galactic News Network.

Velitel introduced us with a surprisingly relaxed demeanor considering he had absolutely no case to present. Uz and Jidlaph raised eyebrows (although with Uz's heavy fur, it was hard to tell) as Nikki and Marlowe were identified, but neither made any comment.

"Welcome to you and all the beings in our viewing audience," Kothan said.

"It's nice to see you on time for once, Merek," Uz added, eyeing the Beoran warily. He sounded like a fastidious school teacher scolding an often-tardy student. Merek responded with the thinnest of smiles and a nod and then leaned over to me and the kitty cats.

"Some of the Council members can be incredibly insufferable at times," he whispered. Nikki, upon seeing the furry bear-like Kreggorian, giving her new pal a hard time, nudged her brother.

I wouldn't mind pulling the stuffing out of that little fur ball.

Marlowe looked worried. *Don't get any ideas, Nikki.*

"How sweet!" I gushed. "He looks just like a little teddy bear!"

Pardon me while I barf, Nikki relayed.

Kreggor was a planet located on the outermost tip of the shortest of the galaxy's spiral arms. This mysterious world was of particular interest to Association scientists because its solar system rotated in the opposite direction from other star systems in the galaxy. The Regional Science Academy theorized that the reverse spin may be the key to explaining the evolution of the Kreggorian species.

They were a highly intelligent race known for their stealth, cunning, eccentric nature and, most of all, fascination and expertise in the field of Galactic Corporate Accounting. Although little was known about the diminutive creatures, they didn't care for Rock and Roll, detested cheeseburgers and considered quantum-golf — the galaxy's favorite leisure-time activity — inane.

Kreggorians were so weird that their parents and teenage offspring actually got along.

The vertically challenged species feared excessive contact with other worlds would taint their culture, but when word of their disdain for the galactic pastime spread throughout the Association, no one was particularly interested in their civilization anyway.

A Beoran emissary summed up most species' opinion of Kreggorians when he referred to them as: Garata-um-parth. Roughly translated, it means: "weird little dweebs."

"We'll begin with Council for the Prosecution," Kothan announced.

"Representing the Association will be Legal Affairs Assistant M3-31-86," Jidlaph, the Council loud mouth quickly added out of fear he wouldn't get much to say once the trial began.

A four-and-a-half foot tall, gun metal blue humanoid android stood, bowed in deference to the Council and then nodded in acknowledgment of defense counsel, Velitel. The android wore a dark blue suit, white shirt, and a red-striped tie (another galactic constant).

"I wonder if Bablona would consider him a hunk," I quipped under my breath to Nikki.

He's a little tall for her, isn't he? she relayed.

The Association, following millennia of obtuse and argumentative posturing, self-aggrandizing displays, and general jurisimprudence — all of which tended to slow the pace of the legal process to that of a Tzarpathian Root Slug — began employing specially designed androids as legal counsel. The droids' dispassionate approach to litigation proved a welcome relief to the over-loaded Civil Court dockets of most galactic jurisdictions. (Throughout the Association, the use of androids was also implemented in the school board, health care and mental health professions.)

As the robotic prosecutor approached the Council's altar to begin his opening statement, I was frantically tugging on Merek's sleeve.

"I need to go to the ladies' room," I said, as quietly as possible.

"Pardon me?" a puzzled Merek asked out of the side of his mouth, his eyebrows forming a dark gray "V" in the center of his forehead.

"The BATHROOM," I hissed softly, but with like, Valley-Girl like, impatience.

The Beoran glanced up at the Council and then back at me.

"You want to take a bath — now?"

I took a deep breath and slowly exhaled. "The toilet — I have to —,"

"Oh."

Dense was not an adjective usually used to describe Merek. He was merely the native of a planet located thirty-one hundred light years from Earth.

"Back out the hallway — fourth door on your left."

I stood up and awkwardly gathered my voluminous robe, looking down at the troublesome garment and feeling very relieved that I didn't really have to go.

"Be careful," Merek whispered, as I turned to leave. "Don't fall in."

I grimaced, and shot him a "yeah right – very funny" glare. Clichés must be a galactic constant, too. Merek must've sensed my cavalier attitude because he gently placed a paternal hand on my arm.

"Listen, those facilities were designed to accommodate hundreds of highly diverse species from all over this region of space. So, like I said — don't fall in."

I frowned, then headed for the door. Maybe I'd better take a peek in there on my way back. I hustled up the middle aisle of the gallery and out of the Council Chambers, miraculously managing not to trip on my Beoran disguise.

———   ———   ———

"Access denied," Bablona 66-L said, in her annoying perfunctory computer manner. "Proper password identification is required to access the requested information."

"Damn! I should've known Nick would protect this file," I huffed. Now what was I gonna do? I weighed my options for a few seconds, decided I didn't have any and then flashed the computer a condescending smile. "I don't suppose, Babs, old buddy, that you could give me the password?"

"Negative. I am specifically programmed not to divulge that information. But —,"

My face brightened.

"Yes, Babs?"

"I am gratified that you think of me as your buddy."

"That's great, Bablona, I'm really glad." Oh boy, cyber-bonding. I put my hands on my hips and glanced around the starcraft's interior looking for inspiration. "For crying out loud!" I finally griped after a couple of moments of fruitless deliberation.

"Access denied." My eyes widened and I stared at the cybernetic face of blue lights.

"Wait a second — the password is one of Nick's stupid expressions, isn't it?"

"That is correct."

I should've seen that one coming a light year away.

"Okay, let's see. Damn! He has so many of them. Ah — Jumping Jupiter?"

"Access denied."

"Geese Louise."

"Access denied.

"Holy Moley."

"Access denied."

"Well, shit!"

"Access denied."

"Babs!" I snapped, growing impatient and frustrated. "Oh, I'm sorry. I shouldn't use that tone of voice with you."

The computer, surmising I would exasperate myself into a conniption, decided to put an end to the guesswork.

"Although I am unable to reveal the appropriate password to you, I suggest you view a film contained in the data files." I took a step backward.

"I get it — which one?"

"'Murder Takes the Fifth,' Earth Production, year released, 2002, starring Holli Daye. Directed by —,"

"That's fine, Babs. Just put it on the screen." I plopped down on the co-pilot's chair and swiveled around to face the cabin viewer. "At least it's something I haven't seen yet," I said as the movie's opening credits flashed. "Babs, just between us — do you know what's so great about Holli Daye?"

"First of all, Ms. Daye's physical attributes."

"Forget it, Babs," I said, cutting her off. I decided I didn't want to know after all. I folded my legs underneath my butt and settled into the chair. "Let's just watch the movie."

— — —

"Glorioski?!? That's it? The filmmakers expect us to believe that a brutal, sadistic serial killer who looks like a super model is actually gonna say something stupid like glorioski? Yeah, right!"

"Leddie."

"Yes, Babs?"

"Access authorization approved."

"Oh, yeah."

— — —

"Holy Shit! I gasped. "Ho—lee — Shit!" I sat transfixed as the information contained in Nick's secret file flashed across the viewscreen. My hunch was right. The key to all of this was the "others involved" — or more accurately — the "other involved."

Physically and emotionally drained from what I had just seen, I slouched back in the seat and stared dumbfounded at the now-blank screen, trying to digest the file's incredible revelations. My entire understanding of recent history (well, Earth history) had just been blown into hyper-space. It was all too fantastic and, to make matters worse, it was likely that Nick was gonna be convicted and possibly vaporized for a crime he didn't commit. Worst of all — he was just gonna roll over and let it happen!

"What the hell am I supposed to do now?" I pried my legs out from under my butt, massaged the bridge of my nose with my thumb and forefinger and tried to figure out my next move.

"Babs, what's the penalty for killing a clone?"

"The Galactic Statute of Limitations is in effect for all clone-related offenses."

"Excellent."

Finally, a break! That makes one in a row.

"Can you take me to Regulon V?"

"Certainly."

"How long will it take?"

"Travel time to Regulon V is four hours, ten minutes, and forty-two seconds at maximum ultra-light speed."

"Great. We'll go there tomorrow after Nick's trial reconvenes."

"Affirmative."

Chapter
22

IT SEEMED LIKE only yesterday (not due to any temporal distortion in the fabric of space-time, but because it actually was only yesterday) that we once again found ourselves assembled in the Regional Council Chambers for the second day of Nick's trial.

The previous evening had been spent aboard Nick's space-docked starcraft, which was under constant surveillance by the ED. While Nick and I avoided each other, confining ourselves to opposite sides of the ship, the kitty cats slept soundly, stretched out on the cool surface of the aft deck as if they didn't have a care in the universe.

Merek and Velitel were at the Galactic Regency Hotel, wining and dining some Koian officials who happened to be on Baltrus VII for a conference on planetary environmental regulations.

Nick continued to steadfastly refuse offering any information or evidence on his behalf, rendering defense counsel Velitel helpless and frustrated. He sought refuge in his music, spending most of the dismal night with headphones clamped on his head.

After seeing the contents of Nick's protected computer file, I now knew his incredible secret, and couldn't imagine in my wildest dreams how he was able to bear the tremendous pressure of keeping that secret all these years. My heart went out to him.

I desperately wanted to offer consolation, but had to play dumb just a little while longer. If he had any clue of what I intended to do, he'd try to stop me from carrying out my plan — the plan to save him from immediate vaporization.

Anxious in anticipation of my clandestine mission to Regulon V in the morning, I passed the seemingly endless hours by watching a couple of films from the library files. Fortunately, one of the GoGanian 360 movies: "The Way We Warped," was six-and-a-half hours long and surprisingly entertaining, given the length.

"It'll be alright," I said unconvincingly to Nick before retiring for the night. He merely furrowed his brow and put his headphones back on.

It should come as no surprise by now that Furrowed Brow is also the name of a municipality on the planet of Xylos IV where the first Sacred Feast was celebrated.

According to ancient history, the observance of the feast began over four thousand years ago to commemorate the first meeting of an obscure and mysterious cult that would eventually change the course of their planet's history. It was known as the Mirabii Gita which, roughly translated from the ancient Xylosian means: The Gourmet's Club.

Up to that point in time, Xylos IV had achieved a level of technological advancement on par with that of late 20th century Earth. The citizens inhabiting the wealthier industrialized nations enjoyed their automobiles and inter-continental air travel, surfed the Xylosia-wide Web and watched hundreds of channels on cable television. Unfortunately, the planet's underdeveloped countries, representing two-thirds of its population, struggled to feed themselves.

The Mirabii Gita first began when three residents of a middle class Furrowed Brow neighborhood (their names have since been lost to history) decided to meet once a week to prepare and partake in a three-course evening meal complete with appetizers, main course, complimentary wine and, of course, coffee and dessert.

Within a few years, the Mirabii Gita culinary tradition expanded to include friends and family; from there, to all of Furrowed Brow and its neighboring communities. Over the course (three courses to be exact) of the next several decades, the once tiny cult grew into a grass roots movement that spread quickly throughout Xylos' wealthiest nations. Before long, Mirabii Gita political candidates were being elected to public office, running on their party's single plank platform: "World Peace Through Fine Dining."

With Mirabii Gita majorities in power, industrialized nations stopped building weapons of mass-destruction, reformed their policies of paying farmers not to grow food and began a planet-wide initiative aimed at providing the entire Xylosian population with one full course gourmet meal per day (complete with appetizers, main course, complimentary wine, and, of course, coffee and dessert). Financially, this initiative was fueled by the booming business opportunities in farming and food production, wineries, distilleries and the largest growth industry, which had blossomed under the new movement's pervasive popularity: gourmet cooking schools.

War, famine and epidemic diseases soon disappeared. Their collective tummies full, the once-starving multitudes emerged as reborn nations now consisting of billions and billions of new consumers whose priorities had changed from feeding themselves to purchasing billions and billions of automobiles, airline tickets, appliances, and most importantly, TV's and PC's.

Within a few short centuries, the fragmented Xylosian economy was transformed into a viable, prosperous, self-sustaining macroeconomic system.

Association history records a visit to the planet thousands of years ago by none other than Lance Ramalamadingdong and Zadar Ko. They were not only extremely impressed with the Xylosian Planetary Wine Cellar but also took back to Pyxis III hundreds of terrific new recipes. Following this historic visit, Xylos was quickly granted membership into the Association.

For centuries, the sacred traditions of the Xylosian religious establishment and the planet's leading theologians have theorized that the sect's original members were devout high priests and learned holy men, but startling new discoveries by Association archeologists (specifically fragments of a previously unknown ancient text called "Nor's Third E-Mail to the Gregarians") revealed that the founders were in reality: an electrician, a real estate broker and an employee of the Xylosian Department of Motor Vehicles.

Perhaps the most shocking and controversial of these archeological discoveries were tattered shards of an ancient document known as Derf's Fax to the Furrowed Browians unearthed during a recent excavation of the city's ancient ruins. It quotes one of the original founders of the movement, who explains to new followers the reason the Mirabii Gita was established: "We were just getting (real) tired of junk food."

Although its origins and traditions remain steeped in historical mystery and religious myth, the Sacred Feast of Xylos remains, to this day, the most popular, widely celebrated and delicious Association holiday.

———   ——   ———

"You were gone for quite a while yesterday," Papa Bear Merek said to me as we took our seats. "You feeling okay?"

For my plan to succeed, I needed to play the role of a schoolchild feigning illness to get the day off from class.

"Is there a galactic equivalent to jet lag?" I asked, as meekly as I could.

"Jet—lag?"

Nick, who was conferring with Velitel on a procedural point, turned his attention away from him to me.

"That's probably what's bothering you," he said, "this being your first experience with interstellar travel." I nodded slowly and offered my best "under the weather" half smile. It always worked on my mother when I needed a mental health day off from school.

"Yeah, I think you're right," I said, with a faint quiver in my voice. Everyone looked really concerned. Boy, those galactic beings were easy.

"That wormhole expulsion still gets to me!" Merek chimed in. "And I've probably logged more light years than all of you put together."

Only the kitty cats were suspicious of my behavior, especially Marlowe, who was always afraid he was gonna miss out on something. To combat their telepathic abilities, I concentrated on feeling lousy — which, given the cartwheels my stomach was performing — wouldn't be that tough. And, I could also distract the always-ravenous Himalayan with some Beoran kitty treats Merek had given me, back on Ohilibama IV.

Velitel turned the discussion back to the business of the trial and the evidence the prosecution was planning to present.

"The CRAP is the most damaging evidence they have."

"CRAP?" My question interrupted the lawyer.

"Carbonic Resonance Analysis Profile," Merek told me.

"It's the galactic counterpart of DNA testing on Earth," Nick said. CRAP can positively identify a specific individual and effectively narrow the field of suspects down to one — which would be me."

Unless you're being set up, Nikki countered. Everyone paused and gaped at her. Velitel, lacking extensive legal experience in criminal proceedings, and unfamiliar with network television crime dramas, was taken aback.

"The prosecution contends that Nick's Carbon Resonance signature was present at the crime scene and on the murder weapon — a .30 caliber rifle — whatever that is," he said, in response to Nikki's conjecture.

"So they think Nick shot Kennedy," I said.

'No, the prosecution alleges he commissioned the crime and had —," Velitel consulted his comm-unit — "one L. Harvey Oswald perform the act."

I wouldn't have to try too hard to feel sick now. A sudden wave of nausea hit the pit of my stomach when I heard the infamous assassin's name.

"You don't look so good," Nick said. "Are you all right?"

"Not really." I felt like I had just swallowed a raw egg, but managed to stick to business. "How did the prosecution just happen to get CRAP samples for a crime that was committed over forty years ago — on a dinky little Class-D planet?"

"The Galactic Concurrence Department was the source of the CRAP," Merek informed me.

"It's funny how, out of all the worlds in the Association and the thousands of light years separating them, the Concurrence Department just happens to be in the right place at the right time," I said, throwing a log of suspicion on the fire of Nikki's conspiracy theory. (Caution: Watch out for flying metaphors.)

"But who would do such a thing?" Merek asked.

"I guess that's what we're supposed to find out — no thanks to Nick."

Nick looked up and scowled at me like I had just made a disparaging remark about Zadar Ko.

"I know I haven't given you any reason to believe me," he said, "but I honestly don't know who's behind this murder."

I decided it was time to bug out and flashed everyone another "too sick to go to school" grimace. Nikki sidled up beside me.

You look like you're gonna barf-a-rooney, she relayed, reading my thought patterns. She knew what I was planning but played along.

"Yeah, I think I'll go back to the ship and lie down."

"If you get to feeling better," Velitel said, "you know where we'll be."

Taking my exit cue, I got up and started to leave. At that very moment, Kothan, Jidlaph and Uz chose to enter the Council Chambers from the door behind their altar. I froze in my tracks but Merek gestured for me to continue on. With an unsteady gait, I strode towards the exit, hoping no one would question my untimely departure and, more importantly, hoping I wouldn't trip over the stupid Beoran robe I had to wear.

——— — ——

Regulon V, known throughout the Association as the Recreational Capital of the Galaxy, was, as one would expect, an incredibly beautiful world. The planet revolved around two medium-sized yellow suns, and boasted the best year-round weather and the most challenging quantum-golf courses in the quadrant. The average temperature during the day was a mild seventy-five, while the nights cooled to a "great for sleeping" fifty-five degrees. It usually rained during the wee hours of the morning, providing the planet with the necessary precipitation to sustain the ecosystem without interrupting the daytime sunshine. The weather was like this nearly every day of the 590 day Regulon calendar year.

Majestic, pristine mountain woodlands blanketed most of the planet's landscape, making it a scenic wonder, ideal for all outdoor activities. And the sunsets — were glorious! Two gigantic glowing orange orbs melting into Ko Harbor at dusk were enough to mesmerize even the most jaded interstellar traveler.

Following one full orbit of the planet, Bablona landed the starcraft on a space pad adjacent to a striking, cantilevered house built onto the side of a heavily timbered hillside. The distinctive residence, its architectural style unlike anything I'd seen this side of the Galactic Council Hall, was encased in copper-colored atomo-glass. The site overlooked a breathtaking green valley, which had, as its centerpiece, a small cobalt blue lake.

The view was a real estate broker's dream.

"Wow, this is beautiful! I wonder if I could timeshare here for a couple of weeks next summer," I said to Bablona, as I stood outside the cockpit hatch and soaked in the setting's natural beauty.

"Please define: 'timeshare'."

"Later, Babs."

———   ———   ———

From the space pad, a three-story high escalator propelled me up the steep cliff to the entrance of the house. (Luckily, Nick's secret files also contained the location and address of my destination). Unbeknownst to me, an internal signal automatically announced the arrival of visitors. This was fortunate since I had searched in vain for anything even remotely resembling a doorbell.

I was just about to knock on the copper glass door when it opened, revealing a tall and very lovely, exotic looking woman. She had flawless olive skin and shoulder-length hair, the darkest shade of brown possible, a stunning face with high cheekbones, a severe, almost cruel, mouth and fiery black eyes. She wore a diaphanous lavender tunic that hung off one shoulder.

"Who is it, dear?" a second voice, a male voice, called out from inside the house.

"DEAR" was spoken with a distinctive upper crust "Bah-ston" accent. A cold shiver ran down my spine and my knees turned to rubber.

"I'm — ah — um — looking for a friend of a close friend of mine," I stammered.

"A friend of a friend, eh? Well, I've certainly heard that one before."

"I'm looking for — ah — Jack." The exotic woman glanced back over her bare shoulder.

"It's someone for you," she said before standing aside.

From the shadows in the foyer, he emerged. I gasped. On the trip in from Baltrus VII, I had tried to steel myself mentally and emotionally for this moment. Unfortunately, when the moment actually came, I found myself woefully ill-prepared.

He would have been pushing ninety in Earthbound years, but didn't look a day over sixty. He still had the handsome face, the winning smile. Tall, trim, tan and fit, it seemed to me he was in better physical condition than when he first took the oath of office over four decades ago. His hair, full gray now, made him look even more distinguished than when he served as President of the United States. He was wearing a pastel blue golf shirt and khaki pants. His clothes matched a casual and relaxed demeanor.

"Hello there, I'm Jack. What can I do for you?"

The shock hit me like a matter-antimatter reaction. Leapin' Lizards — it's really him!

Coming face to face with the man I had seen only on TV documentaries and in magazines, I grabbed the door frame, steadied my jello legs and fought off the urge to keel over in a dead faint.

His eyes widened at the sight of a somewhat dumbfounded (seemingly drunk and/or stupid) woman standing at his front door. After all, he was still Jack Kennedy.

"Down boy," the exotic woman said tersely before sauntering back into the house and leaving us standing in the doorway.

Before embarking for Regulon V, I had changed from Merek's uncomfortable Beoran robe into jeans and a teal sweater which looked great (I thought) with my sun-streaked light brown hair and Florida tanned skin.

"I'm Leddie Fennhadden and I believe we have a mutual friend."

He noticed my jeans, Levi's.

"You're from Earth," he said, with amazing calm given the circumstances.

"That's right."

JFK looked impressed.

"So — we've finally advanced far enough to warrant contact with the Association." I was about to respond when he flashed that famous Kennedy smile.

"I must say, NASA astronauts are certainly dressing casual these days."

"Ah, Earth hasn't exactly made official contact yet."

"Oh?"

"No — just me."

Chapter 23

"IT S A LENGTHY and complex story," JFK said, casually slouching in his seat and throwing his left leg over the chair arm. We were sitting out back at a smoked glass table several inches thick which rested on a pedestal made of a greenish-silver metal that I didn't recognize. Our surprisingly comfortable "Z"-shaped chairs were constructed of the same alien alloy. This interstellar deck furniture was set up on a green-tiled patio next to an Olympic-sized lap pool. From our vantage point, the scenic valley below stretched out toward a distant horizon.

"I first met Ithan Nek—,"

"We call him Nick, now," I interrupted. "It's a lot easier than —"

"Those damn Selrahcian names!" Kennedy said with a smile. "Nick, huh? That's certainly an improvement."

"Right," I quickly agreed, "not that Fennhadden's so all fired easy." That got a laugh out of JFK.

"Fennhadden, that's Irish, isn't it?"

"Yep."

"Good for you. You know, Nick used to call himself Lenny back when I knew him — don't ask me where he came up with that one."

"With Nick, there's no telling."

My astounding arrival from halfway across the galaxy had forged an instant bond between the two of us. JFK and I were like tourists overseas who happen upon fellow travelers from their own hometown.

"Anyway, I met — ah — Nick while I was campaigning in the West Virginia primary. At a reception, as I recall."

"When was that?" I asked, trying to get a 4th dimensional frame of reference.

"Spring of 1960. I remember shaking his hand and immediately thinking there was something very strange about him." Another smile. "Little did I realize."

"I know what you mean — I had the same weird feeling when I first found Nick's ship."

"We hit it off and he tagged along with us to dinner after the reception. We ended up spending the rest of the night in my hotel room, drinking and talking — long after everyone else had gone to bed."

"Did Nick reveal to you who he really was?"

"Not at first, but I was determined to find out just what the hell his story was and began plying him with vast amounts of scotch. You know Selrahcians like to drink, but they can't hold their liquor as well as the Irish." It was my turn to laugh. "After his tongue was sufficiently loosened with adequate doses of Johnnie Walker Red, he spilled the beans, so to speak. Of course, at first, I took it for granted he was bullshitting — thought it was a helluva joke. Then, much to my surprise, he got indignant — I guess the liquor had broken down his inhibitions. When he showed me his tongue and his fingertips and I nearly fell out of my chair!"

"He didn't show you his — tail?"

"No, I decided to take his word for that."

"Smart man."

"I proceeded to grill him for hours on end about interstellar travel, alien worlds and extraterrestrial life forms. He told me all about the Association, his job and the places he'd been. I have to admit, I was utterly fascinated." Kennedy shifted around in his seat, now draping his right leg over the other chair arm. "Back then, space exploration was still in its infancy — we were just starting to venture out into space."

"You know, you predicted we'd land on the moon exactly when we did," I said. "1969 — I did a thirty-page history report about your administration when I was in high school." Kennedy laughed heartily.

"I remember that particular speech. I hope someone informed the Republicans on Capitol Hill of my prediction. As I recall, most of them never thought I got anything right."

"And nobody else found out about Nick?"

"Oh, no, Leddie." Kennedy chewed his thumbnail and considered the possibility. "I was running for President of the United States. If I allowed wild stories about meeting aliens from other planets to get out to the public or the media, I would have been ruined."

"I can imagine."

"After that night," he continued, "we went our separate ways — Nick to beg, borrow and scrounge enough parts to fix his ship, and me, of course, to the White House."

"When did you meet again?"

"In the fall of '63. Because our technology was so primitive compared to that of his spacecraft, Nick had been stranded on Earth for three years and faced the possibility of being stuck there indefinitely. He finally decided to contact the one person who might actually be in a position to help him out." JFK paused and stared out at a really cool-looking hovercraft of some kind — cruising around over the lake.

"I arranged to have his ship transported to a secret installation just outside Washington. The cover story was that it was an experimental surveillance craft — spy planes were big back then." Kennedy chuckled. "Leddie, you should have seen the expression on my face when I first boarded it. I must have looked like I had just gotten Khrushchev to make a major concession." Jack shook his head and smiled. "I had never seen anything like it — the level of technological advancement was beyond anything I could imagine, let alone comprehend. I remember just following Nick around, inspecting everything, and asking him endless questions about how things worked, what type of power source was used — things like that. You know, I've always considered the exploration of space to be the ultimate adventure."

"Tell me about it. Did Nick's ship have the Bablona 66-L?"

"No, that system wasn't developed until a few decades later."

"Oh," I said, a bit disappointed.

"It was, however, equipped with the latest in galactic medical technology." He paused again, a long pensive pause. "As you may or may not be aware, ever since I was a child, I've had all sorts of medical problems. Addison's disease, scarlet fever, a bad back — all sorts of ailments. I was even diagnosed with leukemia at one point when I was a teenager. Hell, I came so close to dying in my youth that I received the Catholic Last Rites at least a half dozen times."

He revealed the details of his medical history in a straightforward, direct manner. No excuses, no remorse — just the way it was.

"By the end of my third year in office, the Addison's Disease was affecting my adrenal system to the point where there was a real danger of it failing altogether. In addition, the pain caused by my back was getting progressively worse. The only treatment available at the time for my condition was cortisone — to kill the pain. The other alternative was surgery." Kennedy propped his elbow on the chair arm and nestled his cheek between his thumb and index finger. "I couldn't afford to take several months off from my duties as President to have an operation. And it was only a twenty-to-one shot the procedure would be effective. My only option was higher and higher doses of cortisone and I was already up to several shots a day." He shook his head and frowned, remembering the ever-present, excruciating pain. "With the technology available aboard Nick's ship, he was able to run a complete physical examination on me as easy as Earth doctors could take my blood pressure."

JFK sat up and looked me square in the eye. "The diagnostic confirmed my worst fears. My immune system was seriously impaired and I was facing a total shutdown of my adrenal glands. Heading into the '64 reelection campaign and my second term in office, I couldn't afford these problems." JFK sat back and sighed. "It was then that Nick suggested the plan."

"The plan?"

"On my authority, he was given access to the components salvaged by the Army when that flying saucer crashed back in '47."

"That really happened?"

"It certainly did."

The aliens who crashed near Roswell, New Mexico on July 3, 1947 were inhabitants of a planet known as LMNO-P, located on the outskirts of Association space. They were a highly advanced technological society of spacefarers who traveled so extensively around the universe that they were able to rack up over 998 trillion Galactic Flyer Miles. For centuries, the LMNO-Peans were on the cutting edge of lightweight aerodynamic design, computer navigation and fiber optic communications. Many of their innovations were instrumental in helping other Association worlds develop safe, effective interstellar travel.

The LMNO-Peans had only one flaw: they were terrible drivers. They were ALWAYS crashing somewhere. The Association cited the LMNO-Pean Aeronautic Authority so often during the course of one millennium that their planetary ultra-light speed license was, at one time, suspended for six hundred years.

"Thanks to some creative jury-rigging and a lot of luck," JFK continued, "Nick was able to modify the alien hardware to repair his ship. Don't ask me how he pulled it off, but he did. With his ship repaired, he took samples of my DNA to Pratelen Beta-Gamma."

"That's where they made the clone of you."

"Correct — but cloning had been outlawed by the Association for nearly a century."

"Why?"

"About a hundred and fifty years ago, during the height of bio-genetic research, the Pratelen scientists were successful in replicating an inhabitant of Graygo 8 by the name of Dictatan Nolugerger."

"Okay, I'll bite. What's so bad about him — or her?" I didn't even attempt the alien name.

"Him."

"Oh."

"Let's see — an Earth equivalent to Nolugerger." Kennedy had to consider the question for a moment in order to come up with a reasonable counterpart. "Do you remember the Ed Sullivan Show?"

"Yeah," I said defensively. "I liked Ed Sullivan."

"Not Ed — that stupid mouse he always had on at the end of the show."

"Topo-Gee-Jo!" I said, suddenly recalling the name of the incredibly annoying puppet. Why Sullivan had that segment on the show every week was a mystery to me. Nobody liked it and the puppet's squeaky voice was like nails on a blackboard. I took a second to ponder the concept from a 4th Dimensional Space-Time Perspective: Two real life Topo-Gigios occupying the same universe.

"The practice was banned by the Association soon after the Nolugerger incident," Kennedy said.

I exhaled. Maybe there was some intelligent order to the universe after all.

"The plan was to replace me with the clone temporarily," JFK said, resuming his narrative. "Nick would then transport me to GoGanius Alpha and I'd get my adrenal system replaced and my spinal column repaired. I was supposed to be back on Earth in three days. We'd pull the old switcheroo once more and no one would be the wiser."

"What about the clone?"

"He would be brought here to Regulon V to spend the rest of his days doing whatever his heart desired." From the gleam in his eye, I could tell Jack Kennedy relished the idea of an exact copy of himself out gallivanting around the galaxy in his stead.

"How were you able to make the first switch?" I asked.

"Ah, yes, the timing on that was tricky. Fortunately, I had a highly confidential — ah — briefing scheduled and Nick and I decided that would be the perfect time to make the substitution."

I considered the word "briefing," and immediately knew he was referring to one of his secret romantic rendezvous. I shot him a disapproving glance, but remained discrete, wondering if he was aware that everyone back on Earth knew all about his — "ah — briefings."

"How was the clone gonna pull off a convincing impersonation of the President of the United States?"

"First of all, he'd be identical to me physically. Second, he would have my prior thoughts and memories up to that point in time. Our experiences would start to differ immediately following the procedure. The two speeches that I was scheduled to give were already written. The only other thing the clone would have to do is shake hands, ride in the motorcade and wave — any idiot can do that."

I had to admit, it seemed like he and Nick had covered all the angles.

"Frankly, there was another reason I went along with Nick's plan." He flashed me a guilty look. "I knew it was going to be the only opportunity I would have to travel to the stars."

Well, I can't say I blamed him — I felt exactly the same way. That's why I coerced Nick into taking me along. The pull of traveling into space to visit strange alien worlds and meeting even stranger aliens was overwhelming, irresistible.

"The one thing we didn't figure on was some stupid shithead killing the goddamn clone!"

JFK slouched wearily in his seat, showing a trace of his eighty-plus years for the first time. He sat for the next few minutes in grim silence, staring blankly out at the lake. I said nothing but wished I had a strong drink in my hand — something on the order of a Long Island Ice Tea — only stronger.

"We had just re-entered normal space a couple of light years outside Pluto," he continued after a long pause. "I was feeling great for the first time in years. My adrenal glands were replaced and my back felt terrific. I even had my sinuses drained."

"Might as well, if you're going all the way to GoGanius Alpha — wherever that is."

"Nick was manning the helm when we first picked up the news broadcasts reporting the assassination. I couldn't believe my ears. I remember just sitting for hours on end, staring at the viewscreen." JFK took another long, pensive look down at the valley. "I knew the human race was not ready for contact with species from other planets — let alone membership in the Association. Compared to galactic societies, Earth was still in the Bronze Age. With access to that level of technology at our stage in human development, we would have blown ourselves to smithereens before the decade was out. I told Nick to turn the ship around."

I sat back in my chair and stared at the suddenly tired-looking face across from me. I now sensed, first-hand, Jack Kennedy's formidable strength of will. He had faced an impossible decision — perhaps a decision more difficult for him personally than the blockade of the Soviet missiles headed for Cuba, when he alone held the fate of the world in his hands. (Did I tell you I got an A plus on that history report?)

For the good of his planet and the survival of the human race, he had to make the ultimate sacrifice: he had to exile himself in space for the rest of his life.

Chapter 24

"I LOST CONTACT with Nick after hearing about Bobby's death," Kennedy stated simply. "Needless to say, I took the news pretty hard." There was a tinge of bitterness in his voice and I suspected he blamed Nick in part for how things turned out. Inspired by my astonishing appearance, long-suppressed thoughts came to him, thoughts that transcended space and time.

"You know, in the dog-eat-dog world of national politics, you're never a hundred percent sure about a person's motives. I don't care how long you've known them or how close and trusted they may be — you're never a hundred percent sure." He paused for another long blank gaze at the scenery. "With my brother Bobby, I could afford the luxury of being one hundred percent sure." My eyes welled with tears. I tried to remain cool and blinked about twenty times in a row, but could not stop the flow of tears that were starting to stream down both my cheeks.

The exotic woman, who had up until now kept her distance, arrived with a tray bearing two chartreuse-colored drinks in bizarre triangular goblets, and a tall glass of milk. I quickly wiped my eyes.

"I have been remiss," Jack said, emerging from his temporal displacement. "This is Zarena." The woman acknowledged me with the warmest of smiles.

"Nice to make your acquaintance," she said, grabbing a drink and a seat. She joined us with the casual grace of someone totally at ease with herself and other beings.

"Likewise." It was then that I realized Zarena had six fingers on each hand and wondered what planet she was from, surprised I hadn't noticed the extra digits before.

I grasped the strange goblet she had placed in front of me and slowly sipped the brightly-colored liquid. Once again, I was amazed by its wonderful taste. I had to give these galactic beings credit — they sure know how to eat and drink out here.

"Go ahead — don't let me interrupt you," Zarena said.

"I think Nick thinks you blame him for how things turned out," I said, before taking another sip of my drink.

"Nonsense," JFK snapped, dismissing my conjecture. "The decision to leave Earth was ultimately mine and I've had to accept the consequences of that decision." He drank some milk. There was nothing Kennedy loved better than an ice-cold glass of milk — well, almost nothing.

"Look at it this way," I pointed out. "If you had stayed on Earth, you'd be dead."

"Excellent point," Zarena quickly chimed in.

I glanced at her and got the distinct impression that she and JFK had discussed this topic before, and at great length.

"That's why we have to find out who is really behind this," I said, placing my glass back down firmly on the table. "Someone out here is guilty of trying to kill you and frame Nick for the crime. Not only that, but Nick's willing to face the Regional Council — by himself — to keep your involvement out of it." Jack sipped more milk. "There's got to be a galactic connection to this murder," I said.

"Attempted murder," he corrected me.

"Right," I agreed. "Sorry. The prosecution is planning to present a Carbon Resonance Analysis Profile that ties Nick to the murder weapon," I added. "Hell, we didn't even have DNA testing back then."

"Let me guess," Kennedy said. "The Galactic Concurrence Department was the source of this evidence."

"How did you know?"

"Just a hunch."

"How would they find out about the assassination anyway?" I wondered out loud. "Or the other stuff – the policy violations. Nick keeps telling me how unimportant the Association considers planets like Earth."

"There may have been an unscheduled audit by the Concurrence Department," Zarena speculated.

"With the thousands of charted star systems in the galaxy, I can't imagine that Concurrence would get around to auditing Earth for at least another millennium," Jack said. "Hell's Bells! We're not even a member of the Association yet."

"Well, I think our course is clear," I said. "We need to find out who IS behind this." JFK pursed his lips and nodded thoughtfully.

"There has been an air of upheaval in the galactic power structure over the past few decades." He spoke slowly, as if he was trying to put the pieces of the mystery together as we talked. "Nick's arrest comes at a good time. A high profile trial would certainly stir up more than the usual amount of attention."

"Yeah, I know. Nick told me there's not a lot of violent crime out here."

"With Council elections on the horizon, the climate has become very partisan," Zarena said. "Kothan's been the Senior Member for the last century and a half and has always been a strong proponent of adding new worlds to the Association."

"Recently, there's been speculation that the others on the Regional Council – Jidlaph and Uz — have been posturing to unseat him," Jack said.

"Primarily over this issue," Zarena added.

"There is strong sentiment in many segments of the Association to shift towards a less expansive policy regarding new member worlds," Jack said, before taking another sip of milk.

"That's why some of the galactic powers-that-be — those with departmental and bureaucratic support — have started to align themselves against Kothan," Zarena said.

My eyes shifted from Kennedy to Zarena and back again, depending on who spoke last. I noticed Kennedy listening earnestly to what the exotic woman had to say. For someone raised in the old school, 20th Century American patriarchy, where the men ruled the roost, so to speak, JFK seemed to have a high regard for Zarena's opinion. Perhaps his exposure to more advanced species (and his own Class-D Designation) had made him less chauvinistic in his views. And perhaps, being almost ninety Earth years in age, he had mellowed a bit. One thing was obvious; although Jack Kennedy had been exiled to a distant planet, he had never lost his keen interest in politics.

"You seem to be up on the political situation out here."

Jack smiled sardonically.

"I'm still a Kennedy."

"I guess politics is another galactic constant," I observed, taking Nick's axiom as my own. "But what does a crime committed over forty years ago have to do with the political situation now?"

"When you consider the fact that the universe is 12 billion years old — four decades is an inconsequential period of time," Zarena replied. "Galactically speaking."

"Let me call in some markers," Jack said authoritatively.

I raised a skeptical eyebrow. JFK stared right back at me.

"I did manage to get elected President of the United States. I believe I can still maneuver with the best of them." It sounded like the JFK of old.

"Will you come back to Baltrus VII with me?" I asked.

Acting more presidential by the second, Kennedy turned non-committal.

"We need more information at this point," he concluded.

"Jack, her friend, YOUR friend, for that matter, is willing to take the blame for a crime he didn't commit to keep your involvement a secret," Zarena said, pressing the issue. JFK leaned back, crossed his legs and rested his elbow on the table. He nestled his chin between his thumb and forefinger. I couldn't believe my eyes. He looked just like an old photograph straight out of a copy of LIFE magazine.

"Bablona says the statute of limitations has expired on clone-related offenses," I informed him, hoping it would help.

Jack thought for a moment, nodded and stood up. He told us he'd make some discrete inquiries, and went inside.

Chapter 25

ZARENA LANGUIDLY STRETCHED out her long, brown legs and used Jack's now-vacant chair for a footrest.

"You mentioned Bablona?"

"Yes, my — ah — the ship's computer — the Bablona 66-L."

"They used my voice for that system," Zarena said proudly. She leaned back and laced her twelve fingers behind her head.

"That's why you sound so familiar!"

"I own a substantial interest in the Bablona series." Zarena motioned toward the house with her head. "That's what I bought with my first partnership distribution."

"Looks like you're doing pretty well."

"Not bad at all — the company's stock is now traded on the GSE."

"The what?"

"The Galactic Stock Exchange."

"I'm impressed." A cool breeze floated up from the valley and the two of us sat quietly for the next few minutes, sipping our drinks and enjoying the view.

"What has Jack been doing out here for the last forty years?" I asked after a while.

"Oh, boy," my hostess said, not knowing where to begin. "He devoted the first few years to learning to fly a starship. Jack's not as great a pilot as he thinks he is, but he did get his ultra-light rating. After that, he spent a couple of years exploring the Serpa and Orion Nebulae and the asteroid belts around Canis Major."

"Interesting." It was the only thing I could think to say. Pretty lame — even for a Class-D species being.

"And —," Zarena added, with a disapproving tone, "bedding every female species on one, two or three legs indigenous to this star sector."

"Oh," I said. Her candor made me blush. "He looks so young."

"That's because of all the years he spent traveling at faster-than-light speed. Time slows down the faster you travel."

"Yeah, Nick told me about that."

"Jack also became quite an accomplished Quantum-golfer," Zarena added as an afterthought. "He shoots in the low three hundreds." She said this as if I should be duly impressed.

A highly technical and advanced recreational sport, Quantum-golf is like regular golf (as it's known on Earth), squared. The clubs are made of a plutonium alloy, are turbo-charged and can propel the solid Tritanium golf balls several kilometers with a single stroke. A typical par thirty on a championship Quantum-golf course is several hundred kilometers long, and requires extremely disciplined technique for optimum accuracy and distance. Players traverse the sixty-four-hole course in fusion-powered hovercraft.

The way fashionable Pyxis popularized the sport throughout the known galaxy, centuries ago, and became the only species in the history of the universe to successfully combine golf with tasteful clothing.

Quantum-golf was considered the galactic pastime.

"When did you and Jack meet?" I asked, finding I enjoyed playing the role of an interstellar Diane Sawyer.

"A couple of years ago — Jack and some of his star jockey buddies blew in here to Regulon to hustle some quantum-golf and, of course, meet women, drink and carouse."

"Are you from here?"

"No, I was born on Ko, one of the seven moons revolving around the planet Senaah. It's located near what's known on Earth as Ursa Minor." I did a pretty fair rendition of the kitties' wide-eyed-with-surprise routine. I hadn't considered the possibility that a planet's moon could be someone's home world.

"Senaah is a giant planet like Jupiter in your solar system. Ko and the other moons receive sunlight reflected off Senaah, which is lucky for us since our sun is two hundred times larger than yours. If we were only 93 million miles away, like Earth, we'd look like the Molten Lava Beasts on Curmudgeon XII."

"Boy, for a lowly Class-D planet, everybody out here seems to know a lot about Earth."

"Jack told me all about your home world and the other planets in your solar system."

"So you grew up on Ko?"

"Zadar's Radar, no!" Zarena protested. "Ko, as far as I'm concerned, is one very screwed up place. Throughout our history, there's always been intense inter-generational conflict among members of my species. Parents and children fight bitterly over everything from personal freedom and privacy to taste in music and clothing."

She took a healthy slug off her drink and I followed suit. Given how relaxed I was starting to feel, I wondered if they contained some galactic equivalent to alcohol. Not that I cared at this point.

"Due to chemical imbalances in the cognitive receptors of our brains, communication across generational lines is extremely difficult and adversarial. Our youth think they know everything there is to know about everything, and older Koians forget they were exactly the same when they were young."

"Sounds familiar," I groaned, painfully recalling the knockdown, drag-out arguments I had with my mother when I was a teenager.

"When children of our world reach adolescence, they're shipped off to the colonies on the moons of Geba and Ramanh. There, they receive their secondary education while working at jobs, building and maintaining the colonial communities. Once the teenagers reach adulthood, they're allowed to return to Ko."

"Unbelievable."

"This system has enabled our society to avoid all that ponderous inter-generational angst and strife other worlds experience." Zarena sipped her drink, and I decided I could use another jolt myself.

"This practice of colonial service was called the 'Peace Corps'."

The statement caught me in mid-swallow. I nearly blew chartreuse liquid out my nose, but managed to keep from gagging. By now, you'd think nothing could surprise me.

"Did you know?" I asked after taking a moment to regain my swallow reflex.

"Yeah," Jack told me," Zarena said, anticipating a reference to the Kennedy Administration's Foreign Service Program. "Keep in mind, Leddie, coincidence is a galactic constant."

"That's what everybody keeps telling me. Did you come here after working on the colonies?"

"No way! When I was the Earth equivalent of sixteen years of age, I hopped a star freighter bound for Regulon V: The Vacation Capital of the Galaxy! I used my natural talents, combined with a lot of hard work and, after a few lean years, became the most successful and highest paid quantum-golfer in the quadrant. After several years on the Galactic Tournament Circuit, I invested in the Bablona venture and, a few years after that, met Jack."

"And you two have been together ever since?"

"You bet." Zarena smiled a feline, almost predatory, smile. "I think Jack relishes the idea of being with the wealthiest and most sought-after woman on Regulon. I drained my drink and peered into the bottom of the glass, disappointed to find that it was empty.

"And don't worry about Jack," Zarena added, flashing an all-knowing smirk. "He'll go to Baltrus VII with you."

"How can you be so sure?"

"Are you kidding? He has a chance to pontificate idealistically before a group of elected officials. Zadar's Radar, girl! Jack'll not only go with you, he'll probably volunteer to pilot the starcraft. You know, PT-109 and all."

"Oh, yeah," I said, recalling the famous Kennedy war story.

"Ugh — if I hear the tale of the old '109 once more —," Zarena griped, "I'll probably slug him over the head with his twenty iron." She downed the last of her drink. "Besides, Jack never could resist any sort of intrigue."

Chapter 26

"THE STARCRAFT HAS completed docking procedures."

"Huh, what?" I had been sleeping peacefully in the co-pilot's chair with my legs tucked in their usual position — under my butt. "What's going on? What's the matter?" I mumbled, still groggy.

"We have arrived on Baltrus VII," Bablona replied.

"Oh, okay," I said, trying to shake off my slumber funk. I rubbed my eyes and glanced around the cabin. "Where's Jack?"

"President Kennedy is located in the toilet module." I sat up and stared at the computer with brow furrowed.

"Do you think I should be calling him President Kennedy too?" I asked Babs, suddenly feeling uncomfortable with my informality.

"Proper protocol provides for former chief executives of the United States of America to be addressed as President, or Mr. President."

"He told me to call him Jack," I said with a guilty shrug.

As if on cue, JFK emerged from the bathroom. He had traded in his khaki pants and golf shirt for an immaculate midnight blue suit, starched white shirt and maroon paisley tie.

My jaw dropped deckward. The transformation was amazing. I could see why, in his day, Jack Kennedy was such a successful and popular politician. His presence upon entering the forward cabin, wearing a very presidential-looking suit, was formidable, commanding.

"Had to dress for the show," he said, with a faux serious look. "After all, Elvis had his white jumpsuit."

"Don't tell me Elvis is out here too?" I asked, not taking anything for granted at this point. JFK shot me a glance and half-heartedly tried to stifle a grin.

"No, Elvis is deceased," he said, chuckling, "as far as I know."

"Come on, we need to get going," I told him, unable to get annoyed at his playfulness. I must admit, when he flashed that smile, it was really hard to resist his charm. "I just hope Nick's trial isn't over yet."

— — —

"The prosecution admits that, although the defendant was not present in the book depository during the commission of the murder, his Carbon Resonance Analysis Profile — present on the murder weapon — does irrefutably and without question link him to the crime.

"Therefore, with the recommendation that the defendant, Ithran Nek-Hånån of Selrahc, be found guilty on all charges, the Association rests. We defer to the Regional Council for sentencing." With that pronouncement, Legal Affairs Assistant M3-31-86 concluded the prosecution's closing arguments and returned to his seat.

"Thank you, counselor," Kothan said. "Since the defendant has declined to offer any evidence or testimony on his behalf, the closing summation — which is the defendant's statutory right — can also be waived and the Council will immediately proceed to sentencing." Velitel looked at his client. Nick somberly shook his head. The lawyer rose slowly.

"The defense, at this time —,"

"Certainly DOES wish to present closing remarks!" John Kennedy's voice thundered from the rear of the Chambers. The Council members' heads shot up from their comm-screens. Everyone else peered back over their shoulders, craning their necks towards the source of the sudden interruption.

"And who is addressing the Regional Council?" Kothan demanded.

JFK marched down the center aisle and squared off in front of the triumvirate.

"I am John Kennedy — the alleged victim of the crime for which the defendant is charged. I will be presenting the final defense summation."

Everyone froze, stunned into silence. Jidlaph, not surprisingly, was the first to recover.

"I find this being out of order!" he bellowed. "Galactic Law requires closing arguments to be presented by either defense counsel or co-counsel."

I couldn't believe what I was hearing. A supposedly murdered man, presumed dead for four decades, suddenly appears out of nowhere and all that pompous ass Jidlaph cared about was proper legal procedure!

"Harvard, Class of 1940, Earth calendar." Kennedy replied, unflustered by the objection.

In truth, John Kennedy didn't attend Harvard Law School, earning only a Bachelor's Degree in Political Science from the Ivy League institution. But we were about three thousand light years from Earth — who was gonna check?

"Be that as it may," Jidlaph countered. "A Notice of Appearance must be filed — in advance — with the Clerk of the Galactic Courts prior to appearing on behalf of a defendant."

"I believe, if you check your comm-systems, you will find the appropriate notice has been filed, received and verified by the Clerk of the Courts."

Bablona had filed the Notice of Appearance via subspace facsimile during the flight in from Regulon V. Kothan, his comm-screen aglow, confirmed Kennedy's contention.

"He is correct," the senior member stated, looking secretly pleased that Jidlaph's protest had been thwarted. Jidlaph snorted and, fighting every pedantic urge within him, sat back without further comment. I rejoined the gang, slipping quietly back to my seat next to Merek.

"Crimony Sakes! What do you think you're doing?" Nick snapped.

"Trying to save your ungrateful Selrahcian ass!"

Hi, Mama, the kitty cats chimed in telepathically. Nikki immediately leaped onto my lap while Marlowe bounced down onto the floor and started rubbing against my legs. Both were purring fast and loud.

"Hi, guys!" I said, stroking my babies. "I missed you."

Of course you did, Marlowe relayed with his usual modesty. He then strutted over and rubbed against JFK's legs.

How ya doing, Mr. President?

"Well, you're a shy one, aren't you?" Kennedy said, leaning down, petting the big kitty. He then picked a large piece of brown fluff off his dark blue pants cuff. Nikki sat up in my lap, ramrod straight, and snapped off a salute to the former Commander-in-Chief.

Sergeant Nikki, Perimeter Patrol, reporting for duty, sir.

"At ease," Jack ordered, shrugging his shoulders. I had told him — or more accurately — warned him about my two irrepressible interplanetary pusses, while en route to Baltrus VII.

"This is Jack Kennedy," I announced, introducing my new interstellar buddy.

"Merek." The Beoran said, remembering to shake his right hand. "This is quite a shock, to say the least. We've spent the last few days listening to the prosecution explain, in ponderous detail, how Nick had you killed."

"I'm especially glad to make your acquaintance," Velitel said, also offering Kennedy his hand. At this moment, he was probably the most relieved being this side of the Zaavan Nebula.

"Counselor." Jack acknowledged the attorney with the Selrahcian "sock on the jaw" greeting. Velitel was impressed.

"Our client has steadfastly refused to allow me to properly defend him."

"That will no longer be a problem," JFK said with confidence. He then turned towards Nick. "It's been a long time — Lenny ."

"Jack, I'm really sorry Leddie dragged you into this mess." The former President (or was he still, technically, the chief executive?) placed his hand on Nick's shoulder.

"Nonsense, it's high time we determine who is actually responsible for trying to kill me and frame you for the crime." Then, a classic Kennedy grin appeared. "Besides, it's peak season back on Regulon." He shook his head. "Space arks full of those obnoxious Aurgurian tourists, in their gaudy spacewear, taking all the good tee times — it's far too depressing." True affection flashed in Nick's eyes.

"Thanks, Jack. Thanks a lot."

Up to this point, the Council trio had watched Kennedy's incredible appearance in astonished silence. Kothan loudly cleared his throat, but Jidlaph spoke first, beating him to the punch.

"If the 1st Millennial Galactic Reunion is finished," he said as sarcastically as possible, "may we continue?"

"Of course," Velitel replied, recovering his courtroom demeanor. "The defense offers its sincere apologies for the delay." He motioned to JFK. Kennedy slowly approached the Council's imposing altar.

Back to business.

"Members of the Regional Council, I would first like to offer into evidence – Defense Exhibit 'A' — myself. He spread both arms out from his sides and did a slow 360 allowing the Council a long look. "As you can see, I am alive and well."

"Can you verify who you say you are?" The question was posed by the usually reserved Uz, the third member of the tribunal.

"The defense has prepared a DNA analysis which we are prepared to enter into evidence as Exhibit 'B' — if there are no objections." The legal affairs droid rose.

"Galactic Rules of Procedure do not provide for the submission of evidence during closing arguments." Kothan, Jidlaph and Uz immediately began whispering among themselves. Jidlaph monopolized the discussion while Uz just nodded. Following several minutes of highly-charged debate, Kothan ended the side bar with a curt wave of his hand.

"Given the extraordinary appearance of the crime's purported victim — the Council will allow the defense to submit these exhibits into evidence," he ruled, to the apparent dissatisfaction of his cohorts.

"Thank you," JFK said, staring straight at Kothan. "Secondly, the defense is prepared to offer NEW evidence which will identify and implicate those actually responsible for my attempted assassination."

"If you are who you say you are — John Kennedy," Uz inquired, "then who was killed?"

"A clone from Pratelen Beta-Gamma was placed in my stead just days before the assassination."

"You can't be Sirius!" Jidlaph protested, jumping to his feet. "Cloning has been illegal for more than a century."

"To what end was this ruse orchestrated?" Kothan asked.

"While the clone took my place, the defendant provided me passage to GoGanius Alpha in order for me to obtain life-saving medical treatment unavailable on Earth at the time."

"That action in itself constitutes another violation of Galactic Policy," Jidlaph charged. Kennedy was not fazed. He turned toward the Legal Affairs droid.

"Is it not true that the statute of limitations has expired on clone-related offenses?"

"That is correct," the android replied.

"Let the record show the attorney for the prosecution has answered in the affirmative. If it please the Council, may I continue?"

Following a few more minutes of lively debate among themselves, and over the apparent objections of both Jidlaph and Uz, Kothan ordered Kennedy to continue.

"First of all, on or about October 22, 1963, Earth Calendar, a Galactic Concurrence Team was assigned to perform a Level 10 audit of Problem Planet procedures on Earth. This action was taken unilaterally without proper Regional approval. I will refer the Council members to their comm-systems which show that, according to the Galactic Management by Objectives Plan 579443-F, Section b, subsection ii, approved and implemented by the Senior Regional Council, a Level 10 Audit — the most comprehensive audit — was not warranted for at least another millennium, given the human race's limited sociological development."

While the Council members reviewed their comm-screens, Kennedy began pacing back and forth in front of them.

"I will again refer you to your comm-systems. The following is a segment of an old Earth entertainment program called the "Jerry Springer Show." (That was my idea.) The Council members stared at their monitors. The longer they watched, the farther their mouths hung open (although with Uz it was hard to tell).

"As Defense Exhibit 'C' clearly indicates — another millennium may indeed not be sufficient enough time for Earth to warrant a Level 10 Audit."

This time, there was no debate. All three Council members just nodded in agreement with JFK's assertion.

"Secondly, on or about Earth Date 11-20-63, two days before my presumed assassination, an Enforcement Department starcraft was diverted from a mandatory policies and procedures seminar on Uhhichcus III to Earth. This action was also taken without proper Council approval. Furthermore, the craft was manned by only one Enforcement Assistant — not the standard complement of two — as required by Section 6767.67-J, section d, subsection iii, of their departmental policies and procedures." JFK slowed his pacing to an agonizingly deliberate gait.

"The defense contends that these actions — all requiring an Alpha 1 Beta 2 Gamma 3 override authority — were ordered in an attempt to discredit the Problem Planet Department." Kennedy glanced over at Nick and frowned. "The defendant's predisposition towards lax adherence to Departmental Policies and Procedures made him an ideal target in a plan to undermine his department and, ultimately, the present Regional Galactic Administration currently in power." Kothan glanced warily at Jidlaph and then at Uz.

"The defense maintains these covert actions were ordered in anticipation of the upcoming Council elections — the Problem Planet Policy being considered by many to be one of the most controversial of the Association's ongoing programs."

Kennedy stopped pacing and stared at the Regional Council.

"It is the defense's contention that there are forces within the existing Regional power structure whose aim it is to embarrass or otherwise discredit the current Administration in hopes of gaining political advantage." One by one, JFK looked each Council member directly in the eye.

"Forces who oppose the present leadership's disposition towards continued expansion of the Association throughout the galaxy. Forces willing to perpetrate the violent crime of murder of a sentient being and blame another for that crime. Forces willing to commit these dastardly deeds in order to achieve their ultimate political goal of assuming control of the Regional Council."

Jidlaph was about to protest when Kothan silenced him with a wave of his hand.

"Finally — the defense would like to submit into evidence computer logs which contain the source of the policy overrides used to request the premature Concurrence Audit and order Enforcement Assistant —," Kennedy paused for effect, and then abruptly turned on his heel towards the gallery.

"— Avith Skairac's starcraft to Earth two days prior to my presupposed assassination!"

Avith slumped in his seat as all eyes in the Council Chambers diverted from JFK to him. Antage stared blankly at his partner, shaking his head in disbelief. Avith sat up, rigid in his seat and refused even the slightest hint of acknowledgment of the accusation. Kennedy then looked at Nick.

"These computer logs also reveal that the authority overrides were not ordered — COULD NOT BE ORDERED — by the defendant. These overrides were authorized by —;"

JFK swung back around to face the tribunal.

"Council member Uz!"

Everyone gasped, collectively uttering the culprit's name. All heads turned towards the Kreggorian's seat. It was empty.

Uz was gone.

Chapter 27

KOTHAN SLAMMED THE palm of his hand down on his comm-system console.

"Security — seal all external exits to the Galactic Hall and report to the Council Chambers immediately!"

Marlowe trained his big blues on the Senior Council member.

Not to worry, Kothan, he relayed calmly. *Nikki!*

Four silver-gray paws pounded the marble floor at full tilt before her brother could finish his thought transmission.

Which way? she asked telepathically, striding towards the Council Bench.

"There's an exit behind us to the right," Kothan shouted as he activated the door's automatic control.

"It leads to the rear security exit," Jidlaph said, rising from his seat.

Nikki was on it like fluff on a Himalayan.

She hung a quick left around Jidlaph and disappeared through the doorway. Merek turned to Marlowe.

"You're not gonna help her?" The big cat stared at him as if he had had one too many Mahoogalian Indigo Ales.

No way! I'm a lover, not a fighter. I leave all that adversarial stuff to my sister — it musses my fluff.

The door behind the Council Bench led to an inclined hallway illuminated by tubes of red neon that lined the base of both walls. Nikki couldn't see the fleeing Uz but her instincts told her he was headed outside to some type of getaway transportation. She used the long inclined passage to increase speed and close the gap between her and her prey. Unfortunately, she misjudged the distance to the double security doors at the end of the hallway and slammed on the brakes a half second too late. She slid along the slick marble floor and smacked butt first into the wall.

Zadar's Radar! She merrowed. *Uz has left the building!*

She spotted the comm-panel on the wall beside the doors, which was mounted about three feet off the floor. She leaped for the audio control on the panel, narrowly missing it with her left paw. She took a few steps back and, with a running start, jumped again. This time her foot found the mark.

"Nikki's at Exit fourteen." Jidlaph's cry blared over the comm-system speaker. "It's already been accessed."

"I'm opening the security doors now!" Kothan said. They had hoped to trap Uz before he could exit the building, but apparently the Kreggorian had figured out a way to override the security system.

Thanks! Nikki relayed as she strode through the doors at full speed. She took two long, loping strides and was immediately greeted by an imposing maze of Bleeckxian Bonsai that was part of the complex's vast Botanical Gardens.

The immaculately maintained hedge was several kilometers long, eight feet high and resplendent with brilliant yellow, red and orange foliage. It looked like five acres of autumn in New Hampshire, or mid-winter on Coball IV. The hedge grew from thousands of evenly spaced, individual bonsai trees with tiny trunks only an inch in diameter. There was only about two inches of clearance between the ground and the bonsai's bottom branches.

Nikki slowed to a trot, trying to pick up the stealthy Uz's scent or catch a flash of movement under the numerous rows of hedge. She increased her speed, racing down the long first row of the labyrinth, and then up the next leg of the maze. She trained her acute perimeter patrol senses on snagging the slightest trace of the Council fugitive's scent and pressed on. She slowed her pace when a soft breeze yielded a hint of the Kreggorian's distinctive odor.

Uz! Nikki hit the brakes, turned on a Xoian Centavo and dived into the middle of the hedge, scratching and clawing her way through the delicate, but dense, foliage. Nikki was halfway through, teeter-tottering on her belly on one of the thicker branches when Uz scurried past her. She swiped at him with her paw, missing by a whisker as the agile bear-like creature sprinted up the adjacent row. She squeezed the rest of the way through the hedge, bounced onto the ground and turned on the afterburners, scrambling to close the gap between her and the fleeing furball.

Uz turned the corner at the end of the row and Nikki lost sight of him. She raced around the hedge, losing very little speed as she leaned into the turn and prepared to attack as the next shrub-lined path came into view.

Once again, Uz had disappeared!

Nikki stopped in her tracks. *Jumpin' Jupiter!* He couldn't have just flown away — besides, she could still smell his scent. She looked up and spotted Uz crouched precariously in the middle of the thick foliage, his front paws desperately grasping the delicate branches to keep from falling. When Uz realized he'd been seen, he leaped from his perch straight at her. She backed up, hissing and swiping as the nimble Kreggorian hit the ground right in front of her, somersaulted gracefully and bounded up into the next wall of hedge. He frantically clawed his way through the Bonsai and was off and running up the next long aisle of the maze.

Nikki knew that the security detachment should be along soon — hopefully sometime before the end of the millennium. They'd be able to cut off a retreat if Uz decided to backtrack. If only she could get ahead of him. She bolted to the end of the row and ran smack dab into another towering wall of dense shrubbery. *Hell's Bells — what am I gonna do now?* Nikki decided if she could squeeze under the next three hedgerows, she could cut him off .

The bottom of the branches scratched and scraped Nikki's slender back and hindquarters as she clawed her way under the hedge's low clearance.

Ouch! — that hurts! Zadar's Radar — I could've saved Mama the money she spent to have me spayed.

She repeated the agonizing process twice more and then stationed herself up against the wall at the end of the hedgerow. Sure enough, Uz came sprinting around the corner and up the path, heading straight for her. He kept glancing back over his shoulder every few seconds, checking on his pursuer's progress.

He didn't see Nikki until it was too late.

—— —— ——

By the time the security team arrived, a hissing, snarling Nikki had the furry Kreggorian trapped. Every time he tried to move, Nikki's razor-sharp claws would jab him back against the hedge.

Uz produced a small paw-held comm device from Zadar-knows-where, but the lightning fast kitty slapped it to the ground as soon as it appeared.

The security team promptly grabbed Uz by his furry little arms and dragged him, kicking and squealing back towards the Council Hall. Nikki strutted behind the detail, triumphantly bringing up the rear.

—— —— ——

Uz bared his tiny fangs, spit and growled as he was carried back into the Chambers.

"Kothan, you and your expansion policies will have the Association's net profit margins erased before the century's out!" he snarled, struggling to break free from the security team's restraint holds. "We must consolidate our portfolio or we'll drown in a sea of our own Red Ink!"

A disgusted Kothan waved him away without comment. Even Jidlaph was at a loss for words (first time ever). Nikki strode over to the defense table and bounced up on the church-pew seat beside Marlowe.

Geese Louise — what a weird little dweeb!

You can brain-wave that again, the big cat relayed, purring and licking his little sister's neck.

"What a good girl!" I cried, stroking Nikki's slender spine and getting a flick of the tail when my hand reached her buttocks.

"Excellent job," a jubilant Merek chimed in.

Still pumped with adrenaline from the excitement of the chase, my little red-ass kitty cat hissed one final time as the security detail pulled Uz past our seats. He was still grunting and snarling about retained earnings, non-performing asset ratios and capitalization rates as he was dragged away.

Kothan called everyone to order.

"The Regional Council will institute an immediate inquiry into the allegations made by the defense. If this investigation finds that charges are warranted, they will be filed against Uz and any others found to be involved. I am also ordering Enforcement Assistant Avith Skairac to be detained and placed on inactive duty status — without pay — pending completion of this investigation." He popped a control on his console. "In the meantime, the Capital Murder charge against the defendant, Ithran Nek-Hånån of Selrahc, has been dismissed." Kennedy acknowledged Kothan's pronouncement with a deferential bow.

"Thank you," he said, turning on his heel and marching up the aisle towards the exit. He motioned with his head, indicating that we should follow his lead. Velitel gestured for me, Merek, Nick and the cats to get up and leave.

"I believe there are STILL serious violations of Galactic Policy to be addressed," Kothan declared, his voice bouncing off the back wall of the Chambers.

JFK, realizing a tactical retreat was not a viable option at this point, marched back down the aisle and stood before what was left of the Regional Council.

"Ah, yes — I was just about to address those very issues."

"Of course," Kothan replied. Velitel waved us back to their seats.

"This is where Jack gets to pontificate idealistically," I whispered to my kitty cats.

Oh, boy! Nikki relayed. You could tell she had found a new hero.

I just hope he doesn't take too long, Marlowe brain-waved. *I'm hungry!*

"Marlowe, you're always hungry," I said.

Incredibly beautiful and hungry.

Kennedy resumed his summation.

"It is little wonder that there are those in the Association who support Uz's desire to return to a time when star systems existed in isolation, and it is understandable to attempt to recover that feeling of simplicity. But in galactic affairs, the millennia of quiet past are forever gone."

As he had done earlier, JFK began pacing slowly.

"Scientific advancement and technological progress are irreversible. The achievements of a Magellan, the first on my home world to circumnavigate the planet, or a Zadar, the first galactic explorer to make interstellar contact with another species, cannot be reversed. We cannot fight the natural drive within us all to venture out, to seek knowledge, to discover." Everyone's eyes followed Kennedy back and forth as if they were watching a tennis match in super slow motion. "This drive is as natural to sentient beings as breathing. However, the greater our knowledge increases, the greater our ignorance unfolds. Our wisdom can only be enriched by NEW knowledge concerning our galactic environment. This includes learning about NEW worlds and NEW civilizations. If the Galactic Association of Star Systems is to continue to prosper, then it must recognize these realities."

As Kennedy's voice reverberated throughout the Council Chambers, I felt chills running up and down my spine.

"The Galactic Family — as I will refer to it — of which we are all members, cannot be limited to a few species or life forms; neither can it be limited to a select handful of star systems. For we are all inhabitants of this galaxy and thus we are — by natural physical law — all members of the Galactic Family."

JFK stopped pacing and gazed for a long moment at the remaining two-thirds of the Regional Council.

Merek and Velitel looked impressed.

"This guy's pretty good," Velitel admitted under his breath. Merek nodded.

"If it is to survive," Kennedy continued, "a family must be able to grow, to progress, to evolve. And, more importantly, it must strive to achieve two essential goals: unity and harmony for all its members.

"How are we to accomplish these goals? By providing liberty and dignity for all species of intelligent life. These two concepts are the foundations of a galactic society where sentient life forms can live together in peace and prosperity." Kothan and Jidlaph glanced at each other. You could tell they were also impressed.

"Physical law dictates that the universe is ever-expanding — and, so too, the Association must continue to expand. It is essential that we go forth to all members of the Galactic Family — whether they are known to us at the present time, or yet to be discovered — for if we do, we shall, in due time, reap the benefits the galaxy and its many diverse cultures has to offer." He strolled over and stood in front of the defense table.

"Imagine a galaxy devoid of the incredibly entertaining music of Chuck Berry?" The two Council members looked crushed at the suggestion.

"No Chuck Berry?" they glumly mouthed to each other.

"Not only does it have a great beat, but it's also excellent to dance to!"

"Dance to?" Kothan whispered to his colleague. Jidlaph just shrugged.

"The unlikely source of this music? My home world of Earth, a mere Class-D designated planet! Consider all the wonderful worlds and wonderful cultures that are still unknown to the Association and will remain that way if we are satisfied with things as they are." He started pacing again.

"In any society, those with the power to govern are necessarily answerable to those they govern. The Association must continue to encourage and support an all-inclusive galactic community where there are no castes or classes among its citizens, where all sentient life forms are afforded equal rights, equal privileges and equal opportunities under its law. This seems to me to be an elementary and inalienable right." JFK flashed his famous Kennedy grin. "No pun intended."

"Therefore, I oppose those who say the Association should pull back from venturing further into space and I question current galactic policy regarding planetary interference. For, in truth, is that not merely a prohibition to interact?" Kennedy slowed his pace to that of a Bagurian Toe Sloth before stopping squarely in front of Kothan and Jidlaph.

"We are all connected by virtue of being made of the same fabric from which the entire universe is woven. And we are all ultimately destined to interact with one another. Hence, we are all members of the Galactic Family."

"YOU HAVE PRESENTED some very interesting arguments, John Kennedy," Kothan conceded. Even the usually full-of-himself Jidlaph had to agree.

"I think the Association would do well to review its existing policies concerning contact with non-member worlds."

Both Council members had, much to their surprise, developed a begrudging respect for JFK during his summation. "All too often, access to those in positions of authority can seem as distant as the stars themselves," Jidlaph continued. He was about to take off on one of his extended monologues when Kothan derailed the verbosity express.

"I couldn't agree more, Jidlaph," he cut in. "The complaint I receive most often is that government is too slow to respond to the needs of its constituency — if it responds at all." Kothan popped a control and perused his viewscreen.

"I am willing to recommend, AT THIS TIME," Kothan emphasized, "that Earth be scheduled for a preliminary membership hearing on the earliest opening in the Regional Council docket."

"I second the motion," Jidlaph said, his vote representing a Council majority. "And if I may —,"

"This is wonderful!" I shouted, jumping up, clasping my hands together and mercifully saving everyone from another of Jidlaph's lengthy dissertations. "Isn't this great?" I grabbed Merek's arm and squeezed.

"Ouch," the Beoran whined, surprised by the strength of my grip.

"Sorry."

"I wouldn't show too much excitement," Nick warned, motioning with his head for me to sit back down. He shifted his gaze to the Beoran robe I had changed back into before leaving the ship. Kothan raised a suspicious eyebrow.

"Problem?" he asked, staring at me.

"Ah — this is an — ah — significant development in Earth history," I stammered.

"Leddie is one of Beor's leading anthropologists," Merek said, bolting up from his seat. "She specializes in Class-D planets, so naturally she's excited about any —,"

"Fine, Merek." Kothan cut him off. "Whatever." He punched another button on his comm-panel. "I see we have an opening on our agenda for Association Date: GASS 5613. I am hereby scheduling the first of Earth's five preliminary membership hearings for that date." He glanced at me. "I assume that meets with everyone's approval?" I quickly nodded, and Merek and I sat back down.

"That would be the year 2455, Earth Calendar." My soaring spirits immediately crashed and burned, landing on the floor somewhere next to my jaw.

"2455?" I yelped. "That's more than four hundred years from now!" Kothan glared at, what in his mind was a Beoran Assistant Vice President (pretty low on the organizational chart) questioning his ruling. This time, Velitel jumped to my rescue.

"That certainly is excellent news. The defense wishes to express its gratitude to the Regional Council for its consideration in regard to this matter." I slumped down in my seat wondering if it would be a breach of galactic protocol to crawl under the table. Merek patted the top of my hand.

"It's a big galaxy," he said, with a shrug.

"And now, the Council has no alternative but to address the policy violations," Kothan announced. "With all due respect to John Kennedy's persuasive closing arguments — and overlooking his presence at this proceeding as a policy violation in itself — Earth is, at this time, still a Class-D designated planet. The defendant's violations of Sections 518.85 and 1226.58, Galactic Policies and Procedures, are serious transgressions calling for punishment commensurate with the nature of these offenses."

Kothan and Jidlaph glanced at one another and, in unison, punched controls on their consoles.

"Therefore, it is the determination of Regional Galactic Council that the defendant, Ithran Nek-Hånån of Selrahc, be found in violation of said sections and hereby orders he be terminated from his current position in the Problem Planet Administration, with the loss of all privileges and benefits derived thereof."

Chapter 29

"NICK!" I YELLED out the door of the showroom. "I need you to pull the trunk lid off the '95 Saturn that's out near the back fence."

It took only a couple of weeks following our return from Baltrus VII for life at Salvage Specialists to revert back to an all-too-familiar routine. The kitty cats and I bid farewell to our new galactic buddies in a heartfelt scene outside the Spaceport Pastry and Java Shop just before boarding the subspace transport back to the third planet in the JAC-91180 star system. Nick, who had not been back to his native Selrahc in over a century, and considered returning to his Tegl-va family only slightly more appealing than immediate vaporization, decided to accompany us back to Earth. Merek and Velitel headed for the far reaches of Association space and their next problem planet after filing a petition with the Regional Council requesting upgrade of John Kennedy's galactic species designation. Jack returned to Regulon V.

I had received a few date invitations from Nick after arriving home, which flattered AND worried me. Jumpin' Jupiter! It was not like he was from St. Louis or Sacramento — or even Singapore. He was a native of Selrahc, a planet halfway across the galaxy. Besides, in a lot of ways, he was kind of an interstellar geekoid.

I decided, after some soul-searching, he could call me and — if I happened to be free — maybe we could go out for a pizza and a movie.

Biff and Chili Breeto tried for months to sell their fantastic alien encounter story to tabloid television without success. Much to their dismay, they never got to meet Mary Hart.

Your mother, First Lieutenant Angela Baztodd, USMC, received her honorable discharge from the Marines following four distinguished tours of duty. With the exception of a wonderful, week-long reunion celebrating her return, life soon settled back into the daily grind that is the lot of working-class America.

"Leddie!" Nick shouted, bursting in from the back lot. "You're not gonna believe what happened last night!" Cheeky was a step-and-a-half behind him.

"You're gonna want to see this, Luv!" The boys hustled back outside as quickly as they had appeared and I stumbled after them, shaking my head and wondering what the hell was going on.

"It's too early in the millennium for this!" I griped.

"Check it out." Nick was pointing to a large rectangular container, roughly twice the size of your average trash dumpster. It was made out of the same charcoal gray alloy as Nick's departmental starcraft. Nikki and Marlowe were already on the scene, heads bobbing up and down, snooping and sniffing the interstellar Fed Ex.

"What's going on?" they inquired telepathically.

"I have no idea," I said, leaning forward to get a better look. "Ask Mister Galactic Association of Star Systems."

We had forgotten all about removing the translator module before we returned from Baltrus VII, so I could still receive the felines' thought transmissions. Marlowe was not pleased.

Nick pressed a digital control on the outside of the container and a pressurized door lowered, transforming into a ramp, which allowed us access to its contents.

Too cool! Nikki cooed. Marlowe backed up, although his blue marble eyes remained riveted on the mysterious parcel. I took a few steps forward as Nick and Cheeky stood aside.

"Babs!" I shouted, immediately recognizing the cybernetic face of blue lights.

"It is nice to see you again, Leddie," the white voice indicator lamp flashed. I swung around and hugged Nick real hard. He grunted something that, when translated from the ancient Selrahc meant: "Ouff!"

"This is wonderful!" I cried. "Terrific! How did you manage to pull it off?"

"I believe the following recorded message will clarify the circumstances surrounding my unexpected arrival," Bablona informed us.

"Greetings from the other side of the galaxy!" the programmed message began. It was Merek's voice. "By the time you receive this transmission, Velitel and I will be on Zagazillion III. Unfortunately, we've got a very sticky ecological problem with one of the planet's major population centers.

"It seems a substantial portion of Zagazillion's western coastal communities were built along an unstable geological fault line which has collapsed into the ocean. Jeepers Creepers! In my hundreds of years of working with problem planets, I've never seen anything like it. It looks like we'll be here for quite a while helping this poor planet recover.

"On to happier things. I trust you are pleased with your surprise. Sending the upgraded 76-M computer system out of Nick's departmental starcraft would technically have been a policy violation, but after our new buddy, Jack Kennedy, straightened out Kothan's slice problem, a Council override was granted. Since then, the two of them have been making the rounds of Regulon's best Quantum-golf courses, when Kothan's schedule permits. His game has improved so much that he and Jack are planning to play in the Pangalactic Zarena Invitational, which is being held on Bagur VII.

"Speaking of Jack, he's talking of running for Uz's Regional Council seat in the next election since we were able to get his Class-D Species designation upgraded.

"As far as Uz is concerned, he and Avith Skairac are currently awaiting trial before the Senior Regional Council along with the heads of both the Concurrence and Enforcement Departments. It turns out Jack's accusations were not unfounded. All of these beings were implicated in a widespread conspiracy to discredit Kothan's administration, depose him and consolidate their bureaucratic power — all under Uz's direct control. How uncivilized! There is also evidence to support the contention that Avith played a major role in the assassination of Jack's clone. Something about a grassy knoll — whatever that is.

"Velitel and I found out later that Jack was able to gain security clearance into Uz's protected computer logs for the evidence we needed, thanks to Zarena. When the Bablona 66-L series was designed, she had a secret universal access code built into the system — a code only she knows — which allows her to pull any file in any 66-L compatible system. Zarena says she considers this access code her ultimate insurance policy. She has sworn us to secrecy and has refused to divulge the code to anyone, including us.

"Well, that's about all the news from out here in the far reaches of interstellar space. As Nikki would say: 'I've got to bolt.' Velitel, Jack and Zarena send their regards. I guess I'll see you guys around the galaxy sometime — whoops — that would be a violation of policy!

"Which reminds me – Velitel and I have put Leddie up for Class-B Species Designation — it was Jack's idea. We've submitted the request to Senior Regional and should have an answer in 75 or 80 Earth years.

"As always, I remain your friend, Merek."

Chapter 30

"HOW LONG UNTIL sunset?" the pilot asked the new and improved, cybernetically enhanced Bablona 76-M.

"One minute, six seconds," the computer replied.

It was a cool, clear, cloudless winter day and the Corvette-turned-spacecraft was cruising over the Gulf of Mexico at about two hundred miles an hour.

"Excellent. Begin audio program."

The twangy opening guitar riff to Chuck Berry's "No Particular Place to Go" erupted over the comm-system and filled the cockpit with what is considered by many beings in the civilized galaxy to be the perfect musical accompaniment for an early evening joyride.

The setting sun was a gigantic orange fireball descending ever-so-slowly towards the horizon and transforming the cool blue-green surface of the water into a sparkling display of reflected gold, silver and hot pink (or fuchsia, if you will).

"This is incredible!" I said, yanking my safety harness taut across my chest and training my Irish blue eyes on the pretty panorama unfolding outside my window.

Nick leaned on the throttle to keep pace with Mister Berry until the custom 1999 Chevrolet Shuttlecraft was just a little silver blur racing above the Gulf's gentle chop fifty miles west-southwest of Cedar Key, Florida.

Since Bablona was physically too large to fit in the limited space of the 'Vette's tiny trunk compartment (and Cheeky really loved the extra horsepower the additional V-8 engine provided), Nick installed the computer's mainframe hardware in my office at Salvage Specialists. He then constructed a specially designed, gigawatt frequency emitter out of three satellite television dishes in order to achieve remote shipboard communication and system operations. (An unexpected bonus was the emitter could also pick up 1500 cable TV channels, including HBO, Cinemax and Showtime.)

"What's that over there?" I asked, pointing toward the windshield at a very large disturbance moving swiftly in the water between us and the setting sun.

"I dunno — let's go check it out."

As the flight's musical director sang something in reference to his unplanned itinerary, Nick eased off the throttle, spun the steering wheel hard to port and proceeded to execute a perfect rolling dive straight for the mysterious patch of movement.

"It's a school of dolphins," I said. "There must be a hundred of 'em."

"Cool beans."

Nick zeroed in on the dozens of dorsal fins gliding effortlessly through the water and the lead dolphin in the group performed a spectacular flying leap that would've scored a perfect "10." (Even with the Eastern European judges.)

I smushed my nose and forehead against the passenger window to get a better look.

"I think they know we're here."

"Well, they are the most intelligent species on the planet."

Our flying sportscar fell into formation just off the dolphins' starboard and, one by one, every member of the group (even the little ones) leaped in and out of the water in playful acknowledgement of their airborne escort.

The blazing sphere, now cherry-red, sat on top of the horizon for the longest of moments, looking like a big flaming derby, before starting to dissolve into the sea as dolphin silhouettes played leapfrog among the gentle rolling waves.

As Chuck Berry wailed a verse concerning the trials and tribulations he had encountered trying to unfasten his girlfriend's malfunctioning seatbelt, the sun took a final wink at the world and the largest dolphin in the school performed one final farewell triple flip, clicking and clacking exactly 71 times in a precise cadence (which in dolphin language means: be cool, don't be no fool) as he broke the plane of the water. He and his extended family then promptly headed for the open sea.

"Bye, guys," I said with a wave out my window.

"Zadar's radar, we're definitely gonna have to do this again," Nick said. He eased back on the throttle, slowed the craft to cruise speed and made a wide, lazy turn into the remnants of the sun's day-ending signature.

Mister Berry finished the musical portion of the program with his trademark flourish of major chords (Ba-ba-ba-bum!) and Nick flipped a toggle switch on the console to transfer helm control back to Bablona. He laced his fingers behind his head and slouched down in his bucket seat.

"Well, what'd you think?"

"Terrific! Fantastic!". I tore loose from my harness, grabbed him by the chin and planted a long, hard, wet one smack dab on his kisser.

Following about a minute of serious, bordering on gratuitous tonsil-hockey, the pilot disengaged from his co-pilot's oral docking procedure.

"Analysis, Babs?" Nick asked, wiping a big red smear of lip gloss from his mouth.

"I concur with Leddie," the computer responded. "Fantastic — or to quote Cheeky — BLOODY FANTASTIC!"

THE END

Postscript

WELL JULIE, AS hard to believe as it may seem, that's the amazing (and historically accurate) story of your dear old uncle nick. And I'll bet you thought he was just very eccentric or bi-polar.

I made a list of the reference sources used in the writing of the narrative. They are as follows.

1.) Personal Journal – L. Fennhadden, dated December 9, 2005 through January 9, 2006; April 15, 2006.

2.) Excerpts from dicto-disc recording – Nick, Cheeky, dated June   19, 2033 (Sacred Feast of Xylos).

3.) Excerpts from dicto-disc recording – Cheeky, dated May 11, 2054.

4.) Excerpts from I-Mail Transmission – Merek, dated August 28, 2054.

5.) Excerpts from I-Mail Transmission – Velitel, dated August 29, 2054.

6.) Computer Logs: Bablona 66L,
                    GASS: 4446.355 through 4447.009
                    Bablona 76M, dated December 26, 2006.

Enforcement Department, GASS: 4446.357.
                                  4446.358.
                                  4446.362.
Regional Council, GASS: 4446.362.

7.)   Galactic Database – Alpha Subheadings: Twany Blend,
       Maris IX, Baltrus VII, Moogalie, Pahoogalie, Nebo-Jaasu
       II, Selrahc, Tegl, Tegl-va, Pyxis III, Procyon II, Zadar Ko.
       Lance Ramalamadingdong (no kidding), Galactic
       Association of Star Systems, Ohilibama IV, Beor,
       Congengabians, Regulon V, Kreggor, Androids, LMNO-P,
       Quantum Golf, Sacred Feast of Xylos, Mirabii Gita,
       Kothan, Symphony Erotica.
       (Nick always used to kid me about how I loved to make
       lists.)

These references sources and a copy disk of the text are currently
on file in a Data Deposit Box with the Mega-Bank of the World. In
a few weeks, the bank will be transmitting to you an authorization
code which will allow you access to the information contained in
the file. Only your parents and I have the authorization code.

Finally, sweetheart, take care of yourself and that wonderful
family of yours. I-Mail me when you have a chance – my new
online address is:

www.galacticallyspeaking.com

All my love,
Aunt Leddie

*****SEND TRANSMISSION*****

www.ingramcontent.com/pod-product-compliance
Lightning Source LLC
Chambersburg PA
CBHW070517260626
47161CB00004B/1571